I0763495

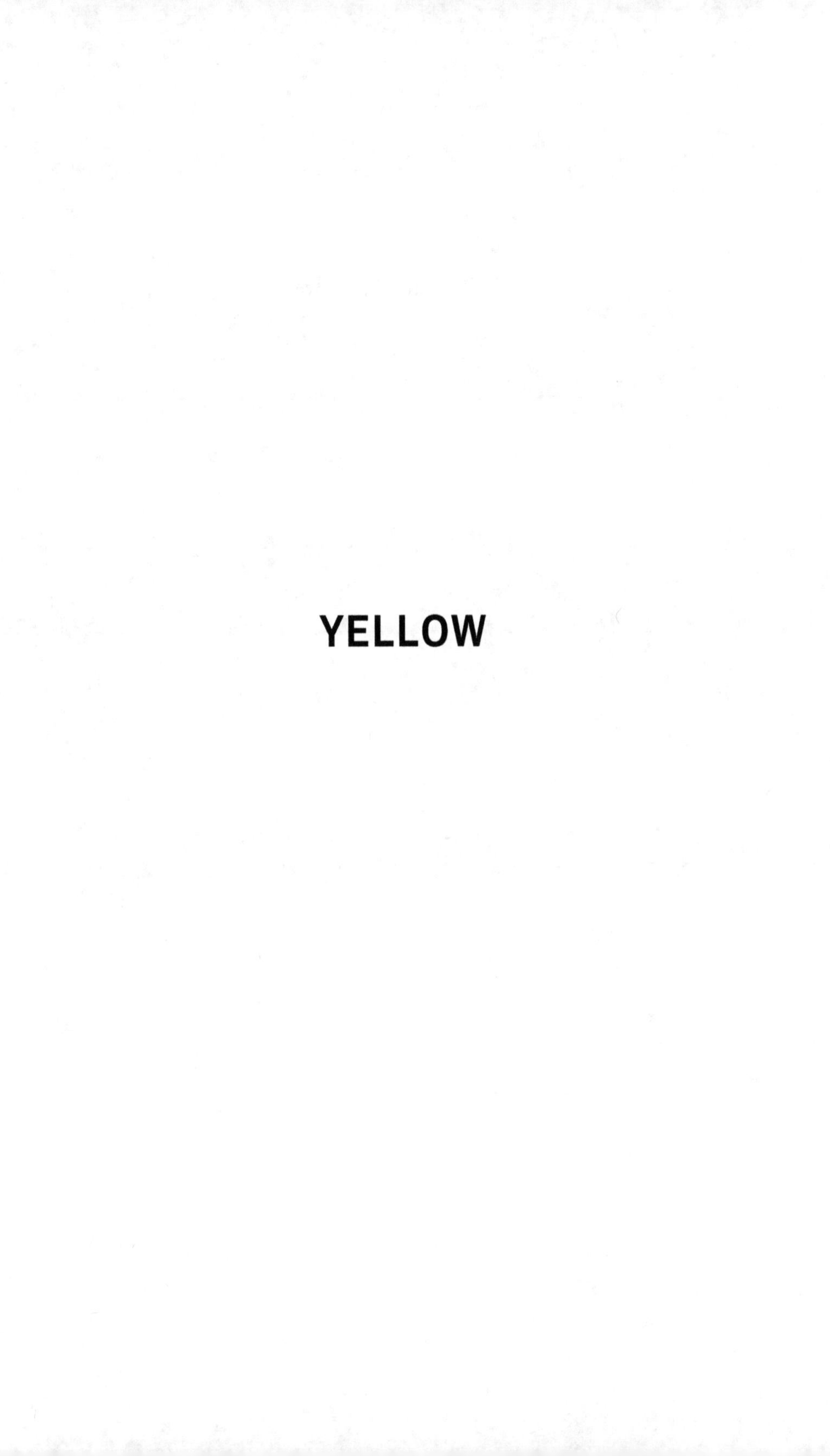

YELLOW

For Daniel J. Tower

YELLOW

A Novella

HUMPHREY HARTNEY

Infamy by Euphony

First Printing, 2023

1

Road Trip

CHAPTER 1

Black Veil

She took another step towards the dark green glow.

A few more steps, then she was over the steel threshold. The coolness of the high-ceilinged room – it wrapped her almost completely in its tomb-like concrete. This was stark relief from the heat she'd just descended from. The coolness, though, was unnerving. It was industrial.

A vent high up in one wall was pumping air. A ceaseless whisper. The room was fridge-like, even with the door open.

It felt as if someone would be there, yet the room *looked* empty. She stepped further inside, started looking about.

Three of the massive concrete walls stood like bland sentinels against her gaze. Along the fourth was a long black control panel. In one way it seemed like a tilted coffin but with tiny lights randomly flashing all over its blackness... All four walls together made the space square, but it was impossible to work out from where she was standing if the room was large or small. It had seemed huge from the outside. But now that she was completely over the dull metal threshold, she saw that it would be uncomfortable for the three people who had to work here – trapped here for the half-day shifts they needed to complete. Sitting, waiting, ready to minister to the demands of the great panel if it ever came alive.

The lighting was dim, all green – but bright enough that she could see the details. There was only one other door – cut into the far wall.

She wondered where it led. This is where they must be... she thought... if they are still here. She edged nearer to this second door. Listened carefully.

She peered in. Heard no voices. Went further in. Heard no breathing, no scuffing of feet, no chair creaks. There was a short hallway with a bench, some plastic water bottles, a microwave oven, and a small fridge under that bench. It was a tight place to make a small meal. Beyond that, there was yet another, smaller door. There were shadowy things in there. She peered further in. They gleamed white. More completely inside she saw what was gleaming - a toilet and a sink. She pushed the door wide open. Its handle hit the wall behind. Metal clinked onto tile. There was no one behind the door. This was the full anti-climax. This was all that there was to so great a secret...

She looked at the sink still trying to get her thoughts straight. The tap dripped slowly. She felt the need to turn it off tighter. But then felt she should touch nothing. When she turned back to look at where she'd entered, she realised how tiny, claustrophobic, and intense this space must be when the main door was locked.

She stepped back the way she'd come. She examined the main door from the inside – it was unlike anything she'd seen. More like some great bank vault door. Dull grey metal. It was as thick as her body. And five shiny pins the diameter of her fists were waiting to punch themselves into the massive steel doorframe. And there it sat, hanging open, waiting to close this small space off against a world plunging itself into Armageddon.

She'd been told that the bunker would be empty. Given its importance, she found that hard to believe, but it *was* empty. She really didn't expect this. In the small hallway that held the microwave and the sink, she thought she could smell the sweat of the soldiers who must have been here – maybe only 30 minutes ago. This smell of human presence added to the eeriness.

She began to examine the massive control panel along the right wall. It was hard to concentrate on what its function might be – and why it needed to be so... long. It must have three parts to it. She only thought this because there were three black, well-padded swivel chairs lined up in front of it. Gamer chairs.

So, this room really did exist. For 27 years it had remained perfectly hidden from... well, from everyone.

Major national spy agencies would have sacrificed battalions of their best operatives to prove its existence. And yet she was able to just wander in. It left her more perplexed than satisfied. But maybe she was just a little impressed – some state secrets really *could* be kept...

She touched each of the leathery seats in turn to see if they were still warm. They were as cool as the air blasting from the vent above her.

She watched the lights on the vast console live and die, blinking out strange patterns. Unlabelled, or with small acronyms stencilled underneath them, she had no idea what the electronic pulses that passed through them might mean. She watched as more small lights came on, then more and more as if building to a climax that would burst into action. But then, after a while, they all went off again in their own time. Around these lights were three great sets of switches, and above these, sets of grey-black monitors – dead monitors. It was mesmerising, spellcasting to peer into them and see shadows of nothing but herself.

Every screen she looked at threatened to burst into life, but they all stayed perfectly dead. She looked up and saw that across the top of the console, above the lights, the switches, above it all, tilting down at her, was one mighty black-grey screen. She tried to see where its edges were – but it seemed to run the entire length of the wall above the consoles. In it she could see another shadow. It was herself again, but this time from an odd angle. This other woman gazed upwards in a lifeless glassy gleam to the concrete roof, poised like a worshipper lost in a dim church trying to see where God might be. She touched the back of one of the three chairs and watched her hand extend and land in the dull gleam of that great screen – as if it were not her own hand. She looked on, half-captivated wondering what that hand would do next.

Someone must be watching her. They had to be. She looked up to the roof. No cameras. No cobwebs, just gently lit concrete, then darker concrete corners and, again, the air vent pumping away. It was odd that there was no lens-like eye peering down at her as she peered up.

Then she remembered the camera she had brought.

She lowered her backpack off her back, put it on one of the chairs, started feeling around inside the main compartment. Taking photos – shit, she thought – *now* she was committed. Now she was crossing lines. Now, she was breaking the law – now she knew she was about to move from *just* an 'accidental' trespasser to an active gatherer of state secrets...

She found her camera. Turned it on. Listened as the lens electronically focused and re-focused.

Then she sat in one of the chairs. It swivelled as she kicked the floor. Click, small turn, click. She did a 360 degree turn of the room taking photos. The light wasn't good. She gazed at the panel through the aperture. Now the great control panel seemed like a shadowy pharaoh's craft sailing over dark waters to the lands of the dead. But the lights it bore never stopped blinking.

Once she'd photographed the room, she let herself relax into the chair a little. Then came that voice in her head again: *why me*?

Annabelle Jones still hadn't worked out why she was the first civilian to make it down here. Why was all this hers alone to discover? They must know by now that she'd broken in. Maybe there were monitoring cameras embedded in the console itself? She studied its buttons, its blank screens... But she couldn't see how they might be watching her. She stood, packed her camera away, left her backpack on one of the other seats, and sat back down again, feeling heavy in her body at the terrifying wonder of it all.

She spun about, then pushed the next chair out of the way with her foot. It shot across the room and slammed into the back wall. There was a mighty crack as it hit. She was shocked at the noise it made and she listened for a response – some other noise. But there was only silence.

There was, of course, an answer to her question. Why her? She was Australia's leading investigative journalist. Or maybe she only thought she was. Who else would have the connections to make it this far? Or maybe she was just the disposable one. Maybe that's why she made it here. Because nobody really cared if she got carted off to a Black Site and was never seen again.

If she made it here because of her connections, then that was because she had made the one connection that really mattered – to Black Veil.

Black Veil was her long-time government informant.

She thought of him again. He was the most careful and precise man she knew. Only a few years older than she was, he was an anonymous force deep inside the Australian security services. He first made contact with her a decade ago –told her about Australian war crimes in Afghanistan. He appeared bearing the proof she needed to break the story. Then he disappeared. Black Veil would keep away from her for years at a time, but each time he found something deep in the guts of government that he just couldn't ethically bear, he'd make contact, hand over evidence, then disappear again.

This was how he'd reached out to her this last time. A few months ago. But what he had to say – it was the last thing she'd expected him to say.

She was delighted he was back on the scene. It had been a calm news year for Annabelle – and for every journalist in Canberra. Nothing. The political desk had been a dead zone. Not that things weren't happening – more uncontrollable bushfires around the world, crop failures, drives to get food to starving villages, floods. But these weren't her beat. She was at heart a political animal and there was very little for her to maul. There'd been no scandals in the capital, no leads worth chasing, no rumours of major government corruption, no war crimes to hunt down, no overseas deployments, no peace-keeping missions to keep an eye on. Nothing but slow progress, well-behaved ministers, and a balanced budget. The government seemed to be running the country under an intended policy of extreme boredom. Everyone who had their hands on the levers of power were being quiet, polite, and mostly out of sight. If this gave Annabelle one thing, it gave her time to experience the strange stillness of middle age. Being becalmed like this was a new sensation. She hated it.

It was intensified by the fact that she and Michael were returning to life without children. Her eldest had moved out of home and was renting digs near his university. The youngest had just completed his Higher School Certificate and had taken off for a gap year in Canada.

And it was in that precisely aligned national and personal stillness that Black Veil made contact again. When she picked up his message her first sense was a feeling of elation that something big might be happening. She didn't know it was going to be this big.

They met in a café in a discrete country town well outside of the usual paths she walked. It was the most unlikely place they could think of: Yass.

It was mid-morning, the café empty except for the waitress loitering near the register and her husband out in the kitchen washing pans.

She walked in and immediately saw Black Veil's face – it was aimed right at the door. She was half expecting that she would barely recognise him. There were no known photographs of him. And it had been years since she'd seen him in the flesh. But there he was, sitting at a table in the corner, back to the far wall. He was different this time. There was something intense about his face, yet somehow there was something more vacant about his eyes – although vacant was not exactly the word... Annabelle looked once more into his eyes as he stood and as they greeted each other. She felt he was intensely present and also strangely disconnected – as if it was all now too much – as if his enthusiasm for being a government man had, at last, killed something significant inside him.

Given the life he'd led and the pressures he'd faced, Annabelle thought it wasn't particularly odd that some light within him had gone out, or at least dimmed. Sooner or later his intense, strange, secretive work would bring down any soul. He smiled wearily at her. They sat back down at the table and instinctively looked about, then smiled silently at their luck – the place was completely empty. After they ordered food and waited for the waitress to wander back into the kitchen, they were alone.

"You're looking *tired*" she said.

He laughed wearily. "Am I? I *am* tired. I know that much. Exhausted...."

Even though his news was extra-ordinary, he wasted little time explaining exactly what he had discovered. Because of the way he mentioned it – calmly and without any framing, she couldn't believe him. In fact, she started looking closely at his eyes, trying to see if he'd been taken over by delusions, by some kind of paranoia.

I mean, who on Earth would believe that a bunker like the one she was standing in at this exact moment could exist? He spoke about it in the abstract, and it remained somehow abstract until now. The room did exist, hidden so far away from the geopolitical swirl as north-west Australia. But back in the café in Yass, she genuinely thought for several minutes he'd gone crazy, or was joking, or was testing her.

Which is why on their long journey to this concrete room, some large part of Annabelle's mind thought there'd be nothing to see when they arrived. Maybe she only agreed to come because she'd get a road trip out of it with a man who'd done so much to help her career... a final tour. And she'd come home with nothing much more than a crazy story to tell her journo mates when it all fell apart... For her, Black Veil had always been a charming conundrum. Maybe this was the strange end to a brilliant and morally-precise life? At least she could document that. But she remained wary.

He had kept his job because deep state power trusted him implicitly, yet by his actions she knew that the government had misplaced its trust... So, and this was something she regularly asked herself, why the hell should *she* also trust him? Maybe she never did trust him– in one way there was no need. He always came bearing unassailable evidence. So, in many ways it wasn't about him at all. She trusted his evidence. Every lead he'd given her turned out to be journalistic gold. But now, in this café in Yass, what he was telling her was simply and purely unbelievable. One part of her was sure he had left reality. But another part of her was sure he was right. He wouldn't open his mouth otherwise. Her confusion grew into anger. If he was right – then the world was damned – how could such a room exist and how could such a facility have been built?

Down underground in the concrete cube with cool air being forced over her, she looked at her watch and thought of him for a moment. He'd come all this way with her. He said it was worth the risk. She agreed with him on that; if what he said was true, this was monumental. And now he was up at ground level waiting for her to document the room and come back up. But she slumped further into the black padded chair. She wasn't going back up. She wasn't leaving. Even though they'd concocted a plan to get themselves out... She knew that in five more minutes he'd take off. That's what they'd agreed should happen. "Wait fifteen minutes – and if I'm not back – get the fuck out of here," she told him. He wasn't a man to go against the plan. She knew he'd be getting ready to leave. She knew she should also get the hell out this very second. Something told her she should run away as fast as she could. This had to be seriously nasty stuff. 'Ok. Time to go. Get yourself back up to ground level,' she mumbled to herself more than a few times. But she also knew something big was about to happen... She gripped the arms of the chair tightly. Her fingers linked about the furniture in case some other part of her tried to flee. Annabelle felt she needed to be discovered here. She felt, somehow, that this was also part of the plan. She was also sure she'd never see Black Veil again.

She began thinking about the form of the story she would tell. She wondered how she could write about it without her readers thinking she had, like Black Veil, also left reality. Why wouldn't the whole bloody country think the same of her as she thought of him in that café in Yass?

But at least she had her camera, the photos. Or would they just take them off her? Would the government just say she'd gone mad? Would they claim that the photos were faked?

Then she started thinking about why she had done all this. All the things that had led her here. All the words penned, all the mad rushes to deadlines, the quiet pride she carried for the two Walkleys she'd won, the institutional sexism she'd spent her life battling. The madness of the press gallery and the parliament. The leaks she'd been fed by scheming ministers. The police raids on her house. The threatening searches to discover her sources. Search warrant after search warrant. The seizures of her computers. Publicly declared outrage against her by the same ministers who originally sent her the leaks... The war-crimes accusations she'd uncovered, the campaigns by pro-military groups to discredit her, slander her, death threats, rape threats, endless trolling... Inside that kind of fury and persecution something had happened. Annabelle felt that she had looked into the eyes of the beast of the state, she'd seen its secrets, she'd felt its patriotic outrage thundering on her back, she'd suffered the glacial torpor of its bureaucratic intransigence, of official intolerance – and she found she was not afraid of it anymore. This is one reason, perhaps the main reason, why she lingered in that black gamer chair.

"This is it" she thought to herself while considering the courage she found in her bones to stay, "it will all be paid back now..." She looked around the room again.

So, she guessed, that if she were arrested, this act would be the state admitting that this room was here. That this room existed. Her very presence in court, when they tried to convict her, would be her safest way to break the news about this room, its existence, its purpose. She would have to be believed when ministers used their prerogatives to shut the public out of the court and seal the judgement. Closed courts were the rarest of events in Australia, the rumours would buzz like blowflies. She looked around again, still in wonder. This room, these photographs, this moment – this all added up, she suddenly realised, as the peak of her career. In the most tranquil, the most boring year of her life, she'd just walked into the greatest story she would ever write. As she sat in the chair a kind of wellness engulfed her heart. She was never more a journalist than in this moment and, she felt, this was also the end of her career. Once this story had broken, there would be no point writing a single extra word. This was the news story that would never be topped, not by her, not by any of her colleagues...

She swivelled about in the chair. She ran her hand along the metal edge of the central console. It was freezing cold against her fingertips –

thanks to the unstoppable enthusiasm of the air conditioner everything was cold and strange here. She got up again, walked around and sat on the chair that had hit the wall. She tried a new perspective. She tried again to make some sense of all the buttons and the lights on the console. From her new position, a cool blast of air crashed against the top of her skull like an invisible waterfall. It was nothing like the heat outside...

Now she was remembering the point at which she was sure he'd gone completely mad. Mad in a deserted café in Yass. He leaned over the table, put his hand on the back of hers for emphasis, and said "I can get you in."

"Bullshit" she spat back at him. She was angry and confused at his revelation, and when he said he could show her the room...take her there... she felt as though he was playing with her.

* * *

After meeting Black Veil in Darwin a few days ago, the two of them had driven South and West. A long way West.

And now here she was, in the room that she thought, back then, was nothing more than the delusion of a man who, after a lifetime of intense pressure, had broken his sharp mind.

They crossed out of the Northern Territory and into the top end of Western Australia. They were trying to avoid detection by driving a ute that had a tiny campervan unit welded onto its back tray. They were now completely self-sufficient. Eventually, they made it to this nondescript little town. A glorified truck stop that sat on the edge of an unassuming military base. A base that had lax security and wasn't much more than an airstrip for the refuelling of coastal-patrol aircraft used to monitor the possible arrival of refugee-filled dinghies.

Just off the main street of the town, he had taken her behind a single-story building. It had been constructed well outside the base's fence line. The building was unremarkable. On the south side it had a long brick wall painted white; this wall was full of windows. Through those windows she could see people sitting in the waiting room of what was clearly a health clinic. There was a solid brick wall on the north side. No windows here. The amount of graffiti sprayed across it gave it a shady look. The wall had a modest single metal door halfway along it – hard to see at first because it was also covered in graffiti. It was a boring little single metal door. It was the kind of door that looked like it let you in to an electricity panel or a shallow room full of plumbing, or it could have been a badly maintained fire exit. But this was *the* door.

The health clinic was the military's way of interacting with the Indigenous communities in the area. Military doctors – American and Australian – would volunteer to treat the locals. The free treatment and high standards worked its own wonders for public relations. But she supposed some of the "doctors" who turned up in shifts didn't stay above ground but came down the internal staircase to monitor this huge panel, keep it primed.

When Black Veil whispered to her "I can get you in," she felt the floor of that café in Yass fall away from her feet.

She told no one where she was going. Not even Michael. If what Black Veil said was true, it was enough to ruin careers and lives, rewrite history – maybe even lead to the fall of the government. She said nothing. She let the weeks tick past and only barely remembered that lunch in Yass. But bits of that meeting came back to her when she least expected it...

"You cannot get me in!," she said to him confused by what he was saying. "That would be impossible."

"I *can* get you in – there are two weaknesses we can take advantage of..." The solid downward stare of his eyes into his soup convinced her, yet again, that he probably knew what he was talking about. He looked up at her and into her eyes with a powerful look of sincerity. It reminded her of how serious this was – and of how serious he'd always been.

After she nodded slowly, he continued, "The first is that this command centre is off-base – the better to keep it hidden. We can get to it through a non-descript door in a civilian building – an Indigenous health clinic would you believe..."

She was still not buying it: "But they'd have to keep a command centre like that staffed 24-7," she replied.

Black Veil drank some of his coffee. "There's one day of the year when it's not staffed – well... one afternoon. There's a major basketball game on the base between the Australians and the Americans – it's hotly contested."

Annabelle raised her voice "You're fucking kidding me!" She realised she was too loud and looked around. The café was still empty.

Black Veil shook his head: "You don't understand the philosophy of all this. It's a security plan to hide the place in plain sight. It's got to seem as unremarkable as possible. So, if there are personnel missing at a huge event like the annual basketball game... then unfriendly eyes might wonder where those personnel *are*... Don't you see? It is *more* not *less* safe to have everyone at the game. That's why they leave the room empty for a few hours... You hide your biggest secrets in the open. As a policy of concealment – so far, it's worked brilliantly. For twenty-seven years this room's been there. Twenty-seven! The Chinese and the Russians don't know anything about it – and if they did – you can bet they would bloody let us know that they knew. So, this security strategy is working and the people who run this little base will keep to the plan..."

He tapped the table for emphasis. "And *so* – everyone will be at the game, the room will be empty, and you will be able to sneak in and see it for yourself...take photos, and I'll be there - to get you home again."

Annabelle shook her head "This sounds like a set up – it really is unbelievable. And how the fuck did you find out about all this anyway?"

"It's not a set up." Black Veil whispered back sharply.

He told her about how he came to know. He had access to files that few in the government got to see – but even with his high security clearance – it still took him years to piece together all the evidence. Years of painstaking, careful, clandestine research. He had checked flight paths for particular payloads, discovered carefully doctored invoices, flight manifests, squads of American engineers flown in and then out again. And every document was given the highest security classification – that in itself was odd... "It can't be a set up – because no one on earth could have guessed that I could put this information together the way that I have– and no one knows *that I know* except you."

"What information? I want to see it." she demanded.

"I've got a whole archive for you, waybills, invoices, photos of equipment boxes, records of flights direct from certain Airforce bases in the US, the size of the cargo planes used... it took them decades to get this done. Bit by little bit, randomly arriving, and years in the construction... If it was normal defence equipment, they'd do it more openly – and with far more urgency. Hell... some of the other technical stuff they bring into Australia – they want everyone to know it's here. Knowledge of what we've got is a deterrent. But not this stuff. Incredibly secret. If you look at the documents I've gathered – and examine any one year, or a few years – they mean nothing. But when you put them together over decades – only *then* can you see what's been happening... Only then do you see the pattern emerge... And – considering Annabelle that you're the sceptical journalist you are, if you want to do this, I will let you see all the files first. I'm not talking to you today because I think you are an idiot. The next stage, if you want to go there, is sharing the indirect proof with you. Then if you think that proof is also what I think it is – substantial – then I will take you up there and show you the room myself. No journalist could ask for more evidence *before* they need to commit to a story..."

She continued to look at him in disbelief. He looked at her confusion and seemed to read her mind "This is not about me going senile from the pressure... if you want to look at the files, you'll see I've got a very solid case..."

All this convinced her to at least entertain the possibility that he was right. "So," she asked him "how do we get up there?"

Annabelle listened to his plans to get her into the room on the one afternoon of the year when it would be empty. And, he said with added seriousness, he was coming with her.

He'd never offered to go with her before. She shook her head "We'll be seen."

Black Veil let the waitress clear away his empty soup bowl. "We have to go together. You need me to get you in. That's all there is to it. I know what keys they use on the doors: you can't break in – but I can *let* you in."

She thought about all this with growing astonishment... "This will ruin your career."

His eyes acknowledged the truth of this. "If it ruins my career then that's what will happen. This is my ending. But you have to see how important this is. This is worth exposing myself for. This is what I want to end my career on. My conscience will be clear if I can get you in. And if this all blows up.... I'll take the consequences... I know what they can throw at me."

In all the years she'd known him, Annabelle had never detected a martyr complex in Black Veil – and she didn't see it now either. She just realised, as he had, that this was too big a secret for anyone to walk away from unscathed. Now that the two of them knew, it didn't matter what came next, exposing this truth would be worth it.

"Ok let's do it." She said, even though they could both almost touch the doubt lingering in the air between them.

Then they left the empty café. They did not meet again until Darwin.

CHAPTER 2

Flash Drive

The year ticked on. It was a Canberra Sunday; a slow, hot, rainy afternoon in January. Annabelle had just driven home from brunch with friends and pushed open the back door. It moved silently. So silently that she took great care to close it without a sound. She took off her shoes and drifted across the lino floor of the kitchen in her stockings. Walking through her house like this, she felt like a ghost – the quietness of its rooms drew a feeling out of her that she wasn't completely mortal anymore. It was as though the whole world was empty, and her house was the heart of this emptiness.

She padded down the hallway and looked past the open door of a now-empty bedroom. She imagined, for a second, that she saw her eldest son as a 10-year-old playing with his Lego on the rug. Then she blinked and saw him as a young man, sitting at his desk with headphones on and his back to her, studying. She blinked once more and the room was empty again.

She wandered past the door of the next bedroom. There was her youngest, asleep on his bed, taking a nap. He was on his back with an open book that had fallen flat on his chest. She remembered taking it out of his hands and putting it on his desk as the afternoon sun slid down between the slats of the venetian blinds. She blinked. Now he was in Montreal learning French and staying with a Quebec family who seemed to have a special gift for happiness. It burst through all the Zoom calls she took from him as they cheered in the background.

The next room down the hall was her home office – only a few meters wide – one of the smallest rooms in the house. She leaned against the door and watched as several suited men pulled apart every drawer and every filing cabinet in the room. It was hard not to laugh. Like a comedy act, they kept getting in each other's way. They picked up every item they could, turned it over, thought slowly about it, bumped into someone, looked about, then either put it aside or put it in an evidence bag and bumped into someone else as they did this. Then she stopped laughing. It was also an abominable sight – three broad-shouldered, dark-suited men doing everything they could to turn her life upside-down... But they were bumping into each other over and over again. Keystone cops. She smiled at the memory of the scene while a shiver also ran through her. She blinked. The room was empty now. No Federal police blocked her view from the doorway to the window. Everything was put back in its normal place. Still, it was hard to look at this room without seeing it full of AFP agents tearing through her life's work, looking for something that might condemn her.

Her own bedroom was empty. She walked through it and the wardrobe mirror caught her movements. She looked at the figure in the mirror as if it was a painting or a photograph that had, somehow, been granted the gift of self-animation. She slid open the wardrobe and took out a pair of sneakers. The wardrobe door made no sound. The silence of the world continued.

Not wishing to disturb that silence one bit, she carefully placed her shoes by the front door. From there she could peer into the dining room.

Michael was sitting at the dining table making notes from a tatty, ancient cookbook. She looked at him in profile, his head angled down, his tall, lanky body unmoving, his back curved over the book before him, his eyes darting quickly back and forth across its opened page. Michael was an intense man. His whole being was concentrated on the words before him as if these were *the* only words that could ever matter to him. Like everything else in the house, he made no noise. This is what Michael did – he studied cookbooks. Then he published research papers on what those cookbooks had to say about life, attitudes, economic supply chains, nutritional assumptions.... "Encoded in each cookbook ever produced..." he would carefully explain to strangers who asked "...is all that you need to know about the history and sociology of the people for whom the cookbook was written." Like her, Michael missed no detail. They had this in common.

Watching him possessed by the book he was holding made Annabelle feel the most ghostly she had felt in years. For a long time, she studied the scene. And perhaps she closed her eyes a little too long, or maybe a little too loudly, because when she opened them again, he was looking at her.

"I didn't hear you come home."

Annabelle smiled at him and realised she was a ghost no longer. She wondered out loud: "Do you think we should downsize..." she asked him, "...get one of those little lakeside apartments in Kingston?"

Michael was not expecting this comment and, being very comfortable working at the dining table simply said "No, not yet."

Annabelle smiled at his stubbornness. She found it endearing, but then remembered what she needed to do today.

"Listen..." she asked him. "Can we go for a walk?"

He looked at her a little strangely. "I was going to make some tea..." he said and stood up, moving towards the kitchen.

"No," she countered. "I really, really, want to go for a walk..."

Annabelle and Michael had many code words between them. Two 'really's in a sentence meant that this was important and had something to do with work. "I'll get my shoes then," he said, changing direction.

It was hard to believe that the house was still bugged, but Annabelle had taught herself to act as if it were. These small paranoias had become strange but comforting habits between them.

As she was putting on her own shoes, she checked the pocket of her coat to make sure the flash drive was still there. Black Veil had left it for her. He'd hidden it in a spot they used so they could swap information. She'd picked it up that morning before brunch.

The sky was overcast, but the rain held off as they made it to the end of the street in silence. As she and Michael approached the park, Annabelle asked, "Do you know where my old laptop is?"

He was looking at a magpie that seemed to be following them. "It's in the shed, isn't it?" he replied vacantly.

She reached out and touched his hand to get him to focus. "No, I mean the *old* laptop."

He looked at her with confusion for a second, then realised what she meant. "Oh...*that* laptop. You'll never guess where I hid it..."

She let go of his hand and smiled. "Well, you can tell me now..."

"We had some scholars visiting from Sweden a few years back, and I got them a temporary office. I kept the key we made for them. I used this to get into the office one night, and I hid your laptop in a little access nook behind a ratty old disconnected sink that's in there – unscrewed the panel, put it in, screwed it all back up again... no one would ever look – the office is being used now by some professor of Media Studies..."

"Does he work on a Sunday?" Annabelle asked.

It took Michael a little while to work out what this question meant... "Ah, you want me to get the laptop now?"

"Yes please."

"Important, is it?" he asked.

"*The most* important" Annabelle obliquely explained.

The use of the superlative here was more code between them. It suggested that Michael ask no more questions. They'd decided years ago that she needed to protect him and the boys from her more sensitive research. It was best that Michael knew nothing about Annabelle's work until it was published. He was fine with that. But now she was half-content that he knew she was starting up a new project. He knew how difficult she was when nothing was happening...

When the two of them got back home, Michael went straight to the car. "Shouldn't be more than 30 minutes..." he said. Picked up the car keys and drove off.

Annabelle felt satisfied. The laptop her husband was bringing home was young enough to have a USB port but had never been set up for Wi-Fi. It had never been connected to the web. It was in fact nothing more than a glorified typewriter with additional storage potential, but it was the machine that Annabelle used for her most sensitive work. No one except Michael knew she had it.

As Michael backed out of the drive, she felt her pocket again. The flash drive was still there waiting for her to pour through everything that was on it. It was, she was sure, full of the files Black Veil had promised her. She wondered if she'd be able to see the patterns that he claimed were there when she got the chance to study each classified document as carefully as she could.

Now she was itching to look at it. She could barely wait but had to keep calm. She stood by the loungeroom widow looking down the street. After a while she started cursing Michael under her breath for taking so long.

When his car came rolling down the road she ran out into the driveway and flagged him into the garage, standing by to close the doors behind the car. She saw the laptop on the back seat, jumped into the back of the car, and asked him to pass an extension cord in through the window so she could plug it in. She didn't want to do any of this in the house. He passed the cord through one of the car's open windows and left her there. Annabelle sat in the back seat of the car for the rest of the afternoon. The garage door was locked, the car's internal light soon went off, and in that darkness the light of the screen was all that illuminated her face. She could barely keep her hand still as she inserted the flash drive. She opened the files and documents. She began to read with a desperate fury.

She looked at how it was all done... She could see it happening – with the most sensitive parts shipped in as nuclear waste for the new dump at Kimba in South Australia. She could see through the invoices and manifests and waybills, that large-military loads were making their way to the North-west. Many of them had been loaded and reloaded and moved north as "truck parts." But then on each of these very pedestrian waybills and invoices was the official government stamp "top secret". There was only one reason why bland commercial documents had been made state secrets. The "truck parts" were anything but truck parts.

He was right.

Annabelle was both impressed and overwhelmed. Everything Black Veil had told her, unbelievable as it was, seemed true – and no one knew it yet – but over decades, Australia had slowly been turned into a nuclear missile base for the Americans. *Nuclear*. She was particularly impressed at the extremely slow and random way that the cargo that seemed to contain the warheads had been snuck into the country. She slumped in the back seat of the car and breathed out one great breath – who knew? Australia was now a significant part of the nuclear arms race and yet no one, not the Russians, the Chinese, and most importantly not the International Atomic Energy Agency suspected a thing.

Annabelle hid the laptop in the garage and put the flash-drive back in her pocket – wondering where in the city it could be hidden. She knew that when this got out there'd be outrage around the world – maybe the American-Australia alliance would fall apart. Maybe this story was so big, they wouldn't ever let her publish it... As she walked into the house again, she realised what she was doing would change everything... She found Michael cooking pasta and saw through the kitchen window that night had fallen and that she had barely noticed.

He smiled at her. "Everything's ok?" he asked.

She faked a smile at him and wondered if this is how Black Veil got through his days. "Sure, sure, everything's fine..." She said, realising what this all meant, and still finding it hard to believe that she was now, somehow, at the centre of it all.

CHAPTER 3

Buffalo

It was winter in Canberra when she flew out. But when Annabelle stepped off the plane in Darwin it was, as usual, tropical, with a force of direct sunlight that was almost too much to bear. She was wearing a black t-shirt, black jeans, sneakers, a black baseball cap over her ponytail, and sunnies. She'd flung a small backpack over her shoulder hoping she wouldn't need much.

She tried to survey the airport as she ate a quick lunch in the arrivals area. As she ate, the whole terminal emptied. No flights were scheduled until the late afternoon and by her last bite, the terminal had become a ghost town. She took this as a good sign. After a second coffee, she found a single taxi waiting out front. She asked the driver to show her some of the sights of Darwin. He drove down to the harbour and through the main streets. This gave her a good chance to check to see if she was being followed.

No one was behind them.

She then directed the driver to a bush-themed, drive-in hotel on the outskirts of the city. Here she would stay for a few days. She paid cash at the reception.

Black Veil would appear when he thought it was safe. She had two fat novels in her backpack and was looking forward to reading them.

Night came. She had dinner at a café down the street from her hotel, then took a shower in her room. It cooled her off a little. She cursed the air-conditioner when she finally got it working because it was so noisy. After an hour trying to sleep with it on, she ripped its plug out of the wall. She watched a crappy Hollywood movie. She didn't remember falling asleep but dreamt of nothing. She woke up early the next morning and slowly got dressed. She wondered if she should pack. She wondered if she would see him today. Then she went down to breakfast.

There was no sign of him.

The following day was pretty much the same. But she discovered the local swimming pool and took her novels there, sat by the pool, and got through one of them in between diving into the highly chlorinated water.

She slept better the second night. She was getting used to the heat. She woke up the following morning, got dressed again slowly. Then went down to breakfast half-thinking she'd been stood up.

Black Veil was sitting at the far end of the room buttering some toast. He stood when he saw her and put his arms out. They hugged. He asked if she'd slept alright. After that, they ate in silence. But it was a knowing silence. Now that she'd seen him, Annabelle felt happy that something was happening. Still, she looked about the room. She found it hard to believe that they weren't being watched.

* * *

About 10AM they checked out.

Black Veil had hired an old Hilux ute with a camper van built onto the back. She loaded her bags into the back. As they pulled out of the hotel car park, a road-trip atmosphere suddenly broke out between them. She was smiling. The tensions that had got them this far faded away as the empty roads opened up for them. There was clearly no one about. Annabelle was finally free of the nagging doubt that they would get caught.

Black Veil smiled and put his foot on the accelerator.

He slid a CD into the stereo. He said it was one of his favourite albums. Annabelle laughed out loud. "Didn't take you for a Cure fan..."

They drove on in silence, listening to the music. After a while, Black Veil hit the steering wheel to emphasise his relief. "Thank god for mothers-in-law, hey?"

"Why? What has yours done?"

He sighed in relief and smiled again – "My mother-in-law is a thoroughly decent person – and she's intuitive. When I asked her if I could transfer some assets to her...you know... she knew what I meant. She knew not to ask questions. That was a few years ago now. I've been planning this for years – by the way. I've slowly gotten rid of every cent I own – just in case. Whatever happens at the end of this journey, my family will be safe and well – and that is such a relief...."

"Does your wife know what you're doing right now?"

"About the finances... yeah. So, she must know something's up. But about this trip – I told her I am on assignment. I didn't want her to worry. There's a lot I just can't talk to her about and she's used to that..." He looked over at her "...must be the same with you"

Annabelle thought of Michael back home in the dining room reading his books.

Suddenly he looked pensive, "She's known since we got married that something could go wrong – seriously wrong – me coming back to her in a body bag was always her greatest fear – so..." He smiled again "...if, after all this, I end up being locked away for life on treason charges – well, that's not so bad, is it? At least she'll know where I am..."

There was a long thoughtful pause before he asked, "Have you made 'arrangements' yourself?"

"Michael knows nothing, I mean I usually tell him nothing anyway... but this – it's all too big. He thinks I'm up here for a private conference for business types on how to handle the media... you know, consultancy work..."

Black Veil nodded, "Clever cover...but what if it all goes wrong? How will you explain being carted off by the Feds?"

Annabelle breathed a sigh. She let her guard down. She guessed she'd have nothing to lose by telling him a long rambling story about Stella.

"Stella and I became best friends on our first day in year seven at North Sydney Girls...."

He was intrigued.

"These days we don't actually have that much in common – we don't talk much. Which is good, because the AFP have no idea we're still in contact...

"Friends for life, hey?"

"You bet!" Annabelle said half laughing.

"But because of all the shit we got up to as teenagers...well...we still trust each other completely. We'd still do anything for each other...you know?"

He nodded. "Is that where you kept the material from your anonymous sources when the Feds raided your house? You gave them to Stella?"

Annabelle laughed. "She liked being a very discrete part of the story... Anyway, I've given Stella two boxes full of letters. I finished writing them just before I left... And also multiple copies of the flash-drive you gave me – lots of them. There's letters to Michael, to my sons, to my editor, to a couple of other journalists, to the Chair of the Press Council... There is one set of letters in one box – Stella will post these if she doesn't hear from me in the next 10 days... And then there's another set in the other box – she'll post these the moment she hears that I've been arrested.... So... I've tried to cover all the possibilities... and every letter has a flash drive stuck to it with all your evidence – if something happens to us – the sky will fall in on them..."

"Wise" he said nodding. "Very wise, I'm glad you did that... It makes me feel safer..."

There was silence in the cab for a while. The "road trip" atmosphere died a little as they contemplated once more what they were actually doing – and its mind-bending enormity.

Robert Smith's voice filled the silence:

...show me how you do that trick
The one that makes me scream she said...

The ute powered down the open road. They passed South through Katherine, then turned West towards one of the Ord River crossings that would put them within a day's travel of the base. Annabelle looked over at Black Veil. "Do you think they'll kill us – or at least one of us?"

He stared straight out at the road as he went through his options. "The Australians won't – we don't have an assassination team... We're not Mossad or the CIA... Maybe the CIA will get to us – eventually... But not any time soon. There's only military up here..."

The answer didn't satisfy her. "You know, we're not just taking on the Australian government this time – we're also pissing on Washington from a very great height..."

At that point the dusty road ended in a t-section. Black Veil pulled up the ute at the stop sign that seemed to sit in the middle of nowhere. He took a right, working his way back up the gears with his foot dancing on the clutch. "If you get arrested by the military..." he explained, "the only thing, at this moment, they'll be able to charge you with is trespassing on Commonwealth property... The only thing they can do is take you back to Canberra.... And..."

She saw where he was going, "Canberra is where all my contacts are..."

"Exactly... we don't know what's going to happen, but the only place they can take you to is the one place where you know *everyone*..."

She was relieved to hear this. "But what about you?"

His hands gripped the steering wheel a little tighter as he explained: "When I leave you at the site... and if you don't come back, I'll get myself across town. A friend left a car for me..."

"Should you be telling me this?" She wondered out loud.

"You might want to know how I am going to keep myself safe – in case you're the worrying sort."

She nodded and looked over at him. "Yes, when it's all done, I might just be a little worried about you..."

He looked at her for a second before getting his eyes back on the road. "I'm going to try to get as far down towards Perth as I can..."

She went through what she remembered of his life: "You grew up in Perth, right?"

"Yeah, a few of my school friends turned themselves into mighty fine lawyers. So, I'll throw myself on their mercy and see what happens next... Whatever happens – they're the kind of self-obsessed law men who like making lots of noise – this will be helpful..."

"Court martial?" she asked.

He smiled, "I'm making things really difficult for them. The more they prosecute me, the more this story gets out, the more public opinion comes into play – and I am pretty sure the public is going to be outraged..."

"It will." She paused before getting to a question that had been biting at her attention for months now. "What do you think will *actually* happen to me?"

"Obviously you'll write up the story, get it published, and become the greatest journalist the world has ever known..."

They both laughed at this.

"If only..." She sighed. "No, honestly, what do you think my chances are?"

He counted off her options by raising his knuckles on the steering wheel. "One – you know the exact timing of the basketball game...so you should be able to get in and out before anyone's realised... you will probably escape detection..."

"Unless they have CCTV all over the place."

He shrugged his shoulders. "I genuinely don't know about that. They're trying to make this building look as normal as possible – cameras all over the roof is not going to be a thing..."

"But *inside*" she said, "they *must* be watching me when I go in – that's why you can't come in with me. Once you get me in the first door that's it – you run for your life."

"I understand. I won't make emotional decisions. I'll stick to the plan. 'Wait 15 minutes and then run...' But as for cameras inside – I don't know..."

"So, what are my other options?" She asked.

"If they do have cameras, the Americans might grab you – but they have no authority to arrest you, and they can't sneak you out of there... Like I said, everyone up here is military – there's no CIA, no assassination teams... no ASIO – that I know of... no attack drones... and the military don't kill unarmed civilians... not when they're based in Australia... The only thing anyone can do is hand you over to the couple of military police who are stationed up here... Like I said... they might charge you for trespass on Commonwealth lands, or somehow try to get you on anti-terrorism laws – then they don't need to let anyone know they have you in custody... But either way, you'll survive until they get you back to Canberra..."

She wasn't sure it would be this simple: "They might take me upstairs to the clinic and euthanise me on the spot – then take me out in a coffin..."

He chuckled. "I really don't think so. They don't know you're coming; they wouldn't have ordered the coffin and I doubt their euthanasia drugs are up to date." He smiled at his own joke. "In fact, I'm pretty sure that if they catch you, they won't know what to do. Or if no one catches you... If you make it out of there with evidence, you get to drive our beautiful holiday van here back to Darwin, fly back to Canberra and file your story that way. Then, when all hell breaks loose, the AFP will come for you... but I believe you happen to be old friends with those guys...yes?"

"Well, they know my address..." she laughed bitterly "...and they know all about my underwear drawers..." She raised her hand as if it had a glass in it – "Here's to Australian press freedom!"

He smiled, then added "The fact is – you will *know*. After you have seen the room, you will be carrying knowledge that no other Australian, save for two or three of us, possesses. You will be a walking time-bomb of knowledge. You have that huge bargaining chip – and your letters...

and the flash drives... and I am sure you know how to access the systems in Canberra that will work for you. So, I rate your chances of survival as medium-high to excellent – but your chances of incarceration, in the short term... I think these are even higher. They'll keep that a secret for as long as they can. Once they formally lock you up and charge you, then you'll know that you're safe – just not free. And while you are at it, put in a good word for me hey?"

"I will." she said not sure if this was a joke or a plea.

Now it was his turn to wonder: "Do you think your editor will be able to get your story out?"

Annabelle slumped in her seat and put her feet on the dashboard. "Not at first, maybe never. It will be a very interesting chess game. And I think it will go like this... I turn up with a story that is going to break the American alliance and tell Australians that they are a secret nuclear power. Then my editor panics and phones his contact in the Office of Prime Minister and Cabinet. All hell breaks loose – but discretely. The AFP swarms all over our offices. I get taken into custody. Rumours erupt all around Canberra. If they arrest me – Stella posts the letters I've given her. If they don't arrest me but keep me locked up, Stella posts the other box of letters I've given her. The stuff in the letters won't get published – but more and more people will know what is happening... the truth will start leaking out... And then maybe..."

"What?" he asked.

"Maybe I have some friends at editorial desks at a range of international newspapers who will publish overseas what local papers refuse to print..."

He nodded sympathetically – "I see you've been strategizing..."

She looked over at him: "I mean, I'm not delusional – this could take years, decades.... A story this big can't be published in a day. I know they'll put every sort of restriction on me – and in the short term it will work. But censorship is a messy thing. In this case, you not only have to stop my original articles from being published – but you have to then censor the news that you've censored me – then censor that news as well. And suddenly people are asking what the hell has Jones discovered, and why are they keeping her in a dark cell without contact. But when people start asking why I have been arrested... or why I have just completely disappeared... then a lot of people are going to slowly learn about what might be going on. In the end it is a secret no one will be able to keep – eventually – *though it really might take years* – I will get to write my scoop and get elevated into Journalist Valhalla for my troubles..." She looked out the window at the scrub speeding past. "But it really will take years...." she explained to the passing flora... "...we don't do press freedom well in this country – but at the same time we're pretty slap-dash when it comes to censorship..."

Annabelle kept wondering what would happen until she saw a strange set of shapes up ahead. She couldn't work out what was coming towards the car and concentrated hard on examining what was going on.

As the ute got closer at last, she could see that the strange shapes were buffalo standing on the road.

Black Veil brought the ute right up to them. Only then did they look at the two humans through the windscreen. Their study was quite intense. After a while, they decided to move on. Only as they trotted off into the scrub, did he get the ute moving again.

CHAPTER 4

Last Night on Earth

The drive was going to take a couple of days....

Sometime after 6PM, Black Veil pulled the ute off the road and drove down a small and potted track. The side road was terrible. Up ahead were two broad bushes standing alone against the horizon - they looked like sprawling pepper trees. Annabelle looked them over, she had never been good at naming flora. He was able to park the vehicle in such a way that it couldn't be seen from the road. Not that this was an essential precaution – they'd only passed three trucks the whole afternoon.

Annabelle looked at him the moment the ute was parked. She woke herself from the otherworldliness of the journey: "Shit, I didn't bring any food!"

He chuckled. "Yeah, but you were not in the Boy Scouts..."

"Ah... Always prepared, hey?" she asked as she saluted him with three fingers to her brow and he charmingly saluted back.

He got out of the cab and started opening up the living area. "I bloody hope you eat meat – I got us some kangaroo steaks – and some pretty choice vino – might be our last gulp of the stuff..."

As he worked at setting up the cooking implements, Annabelle stared out at the plains and the ranges to the West. The sun had lost its strength and was clearly leaving them. A cool and gentle breeze stirred itself. She started to feel dumb, naked and somehow at home. This empty world sparked blissful sensations in her skin at first and then in her heart. She didn't feel like a journalist at all, a spy, a conniver against governments...all the complexities and intensities of her life over the last few years faded away and she felt young again, free to do nothing but look. She was now doing nothing but looking at a beautiful Australian afternoon. There was sadness too – that of all the afternoons of her life, this was one of the only ones she was able to really study, really react to. As she gazed at the lowering sun, she felt that she was almost nothing now but a single soul stripped of all complexity, standing upon the enormity of the planet... If the sandy soil beneath her feet had swallowed her at that exact moment – then she would fall without resistance into the sweet and gentle maw of its oblivion. That would be enough. She realised she had done enough. That she was enough. The horizon just lay there gently, it was mighty and broad, and flat like a soft smile. She smiled back at it.

Lost in all these thoughts, it took a while for Black Veil to get her attention. "Hey! Hey! The steaks are done – come and eat!"

She turned around to see that he had set up the camp stove that came with the ute, cooked dinner, put out two folding chairs facing the sunset, and opened the wine. It was all a little too dreamy to take in at first. It was all perfect, except... Annabelle was just a little sad that she didn't really like kangaroo meat. She'd never taken to it.

All she had to do was sit. He put a glass in her hand and a plate full of food in her lap. They toasted their last days together and drank. "Where's this from?" Annabelle asked as a good gulp of red passed into her belly.

"Orange, New South Wales" he said his mouth already full of meat.

"Ah...*orange* juice." She sipped. "It's good..." She could feel it pass down her gullet and seep into her veins. She cut some of the kangaroo, saw that it was fairly rare, stabbed it with her fork, put it in her mouth and started chewing. "Fuck..."

"What?" he asked.

"I don't like kangaroo..." she said with her mouth full, "...but this is fantastic – how did you cook it?"

"Salt and pepper, bit of butter – the trick is to *not* overdo it."

She ate and swallowed and cut herself another slice and realised there was something so good about all this that it was, somehow, wrong.

"The trick is to *not* overdo it." The phrase kept coming back into her brain. She felt like it was a spell he was putting on her. Tomorrow would probably be the greatest day of her journalistic career, and yet, tonight – it seemed like it all came far too easily. Somehow, Black Veil was not being himself. She got the feeling that he was just trying...

...a little too hard.

"The trick is to *not* overdo it." If this statement was for himself – he was failing on his own advice.

Annabelle's suspicions were first raised by the quality of the meat – too good, too tasty, against expectations. But then this was how she worked. Her *real* self, her sarcastic, highly critical, ever-sceptical journalistic self, re-engaged with the situation and divided her mind. She had been able to do this since she was a child, sitting in the lounge room – listening to the stories her father told her mother about where he'd been. Stories that never completely added up. This was the early spark that drove her fascination for the truth. As long as she could remember, she had wanted to know what had really happened... discover that explanation that was undeniably correct.

So, one half of Annabelle Jones's brain continued enjoying the evening, but the other half watched on as this man played out what seemed to be a delicate script of adventure and daring. As she watched him laugh and tell stories, she saw that there was a core element of seduction that held all his stories together. She felt that the perfected narrative of the evening was swallowing her much more intensely than the sands may have done. The other half of Annabelle's mind watched on too. This was the mind of one of Australia's most gifted investigative journalists. It read every poker tell that twitched across his face...

After dinner they washed up in the small sink inside the back of the ute – pumping water with a handle on the van wall. He washed, she dried. They bumped into each other and laughed. Then, he rolled out a swag on the soft sand and they sat and watched the last moments of the sunset, sipping away the last of the wine. From here she was able to leave her body and watch the two of them – disembodied from above and behind. More like an angel of reckoning than a traveller. She watched, external to both of them, as he tenderly brushed the hair from her forehead. As he gazed at her again – just like he had in the ute earlier that day.

Enjoying his performance a little too much, she watched herself joke to him that, "...maybe there's no secret room waiting for us to see tomorrow. Maybe there's no U.S. nuclear plot...." She pushed him in the shoulder. "Hey... maybe there's not even a basketball game – maybe you just told me all those things to get me out here under the stars so you could fuck me?"

She watched herself say *fuck me* in a way that was both an accusation and an invitation. She was eager to carry on with the seduction because she knew no Australian man could be anything but himself when pushed a little too far... The journalist in her wanted to see where this would go and what it might tell her. And so, she watched as he pushed her back on the swag and kissed her. She couldn't help but smile. He was as much of an expert in kissing as he was in espionage.

From her angel's position she watched as their bodies came together. The expert (former Boy Scout) slowly got their clothes off, moving delicately over her body and addressing her flesh like a butcher might – cut by delicious cut. She watched with delight his kind, loving foreplay, as she heard him say again and again in her mind: *The point is not to overdo it.*

His first thrust into her brought her fully back into herself. She remained integral and whole as he fucked her with military skill to an orgasm that shot up and down her body like a beautiful outflanking move on a battlefield. But while he outflanked his lover, the journalist was able to do what she needed to do – she gathered in that funk of ecstasy all the proof she required – she stared into his dark eyes as he worked his magic over her. And while he was lost in that passion, and as the very final light of the sun lit them, she spotted it. There, behind his eyes, were two selves – the first was a man struggling beautifully to create pleasure, but at the same time there was also another doing all he could to hide something. Something essential.

Relieved that the tensions between them had been so beautifully fucked away, she was able to raise herself again above both their bodies and look down once more as his back, hips, and arse struggled and twisted into her and towards his own orgasm. Up there, Annabelle was waiting patiently for exactly the right moment to strike - for she had now seen what she needed to see...

He rolled off her, exhausted, on the swag next to her and they both gazed at the emerging stars. "Incredible," he said as they both enjoyed the silence – a total quiet except for their breathing.

"So..." she asked with perfect timing. "In your general outlook – would you say that, politically, you are to the right or to the left?"

CHAPTER 5

Western Civilization

His flesh shuddered at the question. "That's a bit personal, isn't it?" he asked – a little defensively.

"You just came inside me – equally personal, I think."

"Well," he chuckled a little uncomfortably, "Let me put my brain back inside my skull while I think of an answer...." He ran his hands through his hair and thought for a moment.

He laughed again and explained – "At a practical level, you'd call me a swinging voter I supposed – I'm not committed to any party. I'm not allowed to get involved in party politics anyway..."

"Well..." she asked trying to mine deeper, "what do you think about our refugee detention camps, the environment, the Uluru Statement, vaccination, voice to parliament, colonialism and neo-colonialism, our place in the region, Black deaths in custody – Western Civilisation in general? Where do you sit on the political spectrum? You can speak your mind now – the naked lady is already yours..."

He sat up and the almost-dead sun caught the creases on his face. There was more silence for a while before he spoke. "One of my great uncles was Francis de Groot."

"Ah," she said, "I've just fucked a scion of a right-wing paramilitary unit, have I?"

At that he laughed long and hard. "No, I'm starting there because, it's true, there were a lot of lunatic right-wingers in my family a couple of generations ago. I admit that, and I admit that it's a shameful history – but back in the 1930s look at exactly who de Groot and his mob were fighting – that crypto-Communist Jack Lang..."

She nodded, understanding and he continued.

"I suppose, if you want to know how I feel about things, Lang is a good place to start. In the late 1920s, Lang didn't just want socialism in Australia, he wanted to divorce Australia from the rest of the world. If you read about that history – and I *have* because my family was so involved in it all – that's what the Lang Plan was all about. As much as I am glad that the right-wing nut jobs in my family have been bred out, I'm also happy that my ancestors stood up against Lang and his strange-arse ideas for Australian isolationism..."

As he continued to explain himself, Annabelle was intrigued by the way he saw Australian history - not as a left wing/right wing problem, but as isolationists/not-isolationist issue.

He ran his fingers through his hair and his voice became more tense. "We can't isolate ourselves from the world – for good or for bad, we're English-speakers, we're one of the Five-Eyes, we are a definite part of Western Civilisation. We can negotiate around these facts, and this might help us to fit more into our region and to address indigenous claims... but we can't negotiate them away as if they're not real. We're a former British colony in Oceania built by White people... So, if you want to know what I think politically – then I personally think Paul Keating – who was, of course, the most devoted student Lang ever had – was probably our most dangerous Prime Minster. He wasn't an isolationist – but an *Asianist*. And we can't follow his big picture bullshit. We can't be an independent republic in Asia pretending that we're somehow Asian.... At the heart of our nation, we're none of those things. As a nation we might not exactly be completely white, Christian, and British anymore – but that's the legacy we most closely have to work from... and that's who we are.... Anglophones and Western democrats."

"So, you're in favour of the American alliance?" she asked to the heavens.

He rolled on his side, put his head on his hand and looked at her ruefully. "Yes, yes, I am very much in favour of it – and also, look what we're doing! Tomorrow, I am going to help you do as much damage to that alliance as any single person ever has. Just don't think of me as a completely evil White man in thrall to Washington... I'm not one of those lunatics who's obsessed with America... in fact I'm helping you because I genuinely feel things like the American alliance can go too far. I just don't think Australia needs to be a nuclear power..."

For Annabelle his voice sounded painfully genuine. But now she was confused...

"So there you go," he finished up. "If I am anything, I am one of the millions of Australians turned off by any form of radicalism, extremism, or utopianism... but at the same time..." He left the silence hanging.

She sat up. Her mind had been stirred. Her fire increasing. She was ready to confront him. "Nice pep talk bud. But I don't believe you. I don't know what's going to happen tomorrow – but I think this is a fucking set up." She looked him right in the eyes and said it "...and I think you're in on it."

He spun around to face her sitting cross-legged on the swag a flash of anger passing up his back. "What the fuck makes you say that?"

She was totally honest with him. "The steaks were too good."

Suddenly Black Veil was incredulous. His voice rose several octaves – "What?"

She smiled. "It's a journalist's intuition mate – have you ever been in a situation where things are too good to be true?"

He stopped himself from protesting... "You mean an inner suspicion?" She nodded.

"I'm a spy," he replied. "I work on inner suspicion." He gave a chuckle. But she could see he was feeling exposed.

Then he chuckled again – "So, the steaks were too good were they? – and now you're suspicious?" He smiled at this. "I hope then that the ordinariness of the sex killed the suspicion that was generated by the excellence of the steaks?"

She shook her head and put her hand on his exposed thigh – the better to feel the truth and lies rippling through his flesh. "No, that's where you really fucked up – my friend – and pun intended... the sex was too good as well... up there with the steaks – and the wine... Anyway, the point is now I don't know what to think... I thought I could trust you – I thought when you came and told me that the Americans had snuck nuclear weapons into northern Australia – without asking the Australian people – I thought that it could be the story of the century. But now that you've fed me steak and fucked me stupid, I don't know shit except you are in on something... and I'm being played here..."

He got up and put his shirt back on. It gave him the chance to turn away from her words. It gave him the chance to think about how he could save the situation.

He stood there in the dark looking down at her moonlit nakedness. She was intent on keeping him on edge by staying naked. She got up too and sat back in one of the chairs and just stared at him. At last, he broke.

"Ok, you're right, it is a set up. They threatened to cut off my balls and lock me up for life if I didn't get you up here."

"Who?"

"The Americans, the Australians – they're working together on this."

"Why?"

He put one hand on his hip and barely thought about what to say. "Because they really did sneak nuclear weapons into Australia, and I really am taking you to the command centre tomorrow at 2PM while the staff who run the joint are at a basketball match on the base. That really is happening Annabelle. It is all true. I have brought you specifically so you can break the story. Tomorrow is their D-day for the big reveal. You think you are stealing the story? That's what they wanted you to think. The truth is you are a part of their plan to let the world know that there is a nuclear weapons installation a couple of hundred kilometres from here. That's the deal. You get the story. You get confirmed as Australia's greatest journalist, you get the glory, the notoriety, the fame. And they get to play out the next part of their plan."

She was amazed by the confession and screamed to the stars, "Which is?"

He looked at her confused, "What, their plan? Well – to let the world know that a new level of threat is about – and that if anything happens, Australia can fight back – but after that – why the fuck would they tell me? Apart from getting the news out – through you – I have no fucking idea what this is about – Jesus Christ – I'm a pawn in this just like you. All I know is that they want you in that control room tomorrow, at 2PM. They want you to see it. They want you to take photos. They want you to write the story and get it published and let the world know that it is there. And I guess that when you get back to Canberra – your editor will *not* be stopping you from publishing it. Your safety is guaranteed – I made sure of that before I agreed to this... And they have made this all about you not because they are out to get Annabelle Jones, or lock up Annabelle Jones, or stop you publishing, but because they wanted Australia's most prominent journalist to be here for this moment... for this revelation..." He paused and thought a while longer as she watched his face intently. "All I can assume from this is that they want this story out – that's the only reason I can think of for why they've got me to bring you up here."

Annabelle was amazed – "...why all the subterfuge then. Why make out that this was all so clandestine?"

He smiled at her, but this time wiltingly. "How else would I have got you up here?"

Taking all this in, Annabelle finally got up and started dressing. She demanded to know the full enormity of what she would see when they arrived. "Like, where are these missile silos?"

He went and turned on a light in the van. He beckoned her over to near the rear door where the light lit the ground. He got down on his haunches and picked up a stick and started drawing in the sand. "There are three sites – and they are all off base – the water and sewerage treatment plant on the outskirts of town – it's only half dedicated to sewerage and water – four of the six huge water tanks there are missile silos. Their tops pop off and missiles come out. Then closer to town are two truck repair depots – each has a warehouse marked 'Parts Warehouse'. The front half of the warehouses are full of truck parts, but the other half are covers for more silos."

"What's in the silos?"

"At the sewerage works, eight Nuclear-armed ballistic missiles with eight megaton warheads. In the truck warehouses, four each."

"Fuck me... You said the Russians and the Chinese *don't* know about this?"

He chuckled to himself – still amazed that such a secret had been kept so well. "It's been the biggest secret this century. You, me, the Prime Minister, the Chief of Defence, we're the only Australians who know. Even the Americans who do top secret work in the control centre think they are monitoring conventional missiles. Even they don't know it's a nuclear site..."

She was not impressed by any of this. "Who told you to get me up here?"

"Chief of Defence – I met him at a model railway exhibition at the start of the year. We had a coffee sitting there among those unwashed piss-drenched train spotters, and he explained it all to me."

"Why?" she kicked the ground desperately thinking. "Why me? Why, why, why?"

"I don't know – but they want the world to know. The good part about that is if you tell the world then you're doing exactly what they want – they can't hang you out to dry for that. You're a hell of a lot safer than you think you are Annabelle Jones."

"Safe, am I?" Annabelle screeched. "And you too? You're safe as well? I suppose that story about your mother-in-law, and divesting assets, and hot-tailing it to Perth was a pile of horseshit?"

Now Black Veil was embarrassed by all that. "Yeah, after I leave you, I walk onto the base and they fly me back to Canberra, I file a report about this, do a couple of debrief sessions and take early retirement."

"So, your mother-in-law doesn't have all your cash under her pillow?"

"No – when I get back to the ACT, I get my super paid out early and, instead of court-martialling me for releasing state secrets to you, I get a pardon for my sins of talking to you about the war crimes. I get a new identity and a new life. It's the end. You'll never see me again."

"That's a shame..." she shook her head.

"Why?"

Annabelle tapped his knee with her foot. "Because you sure know how to wine and dine a lady!"

Black Veil looked at her quizzically. "Is that a compliment, or more of your delightful sarcasm?"

CHAPTER 6

Coro a bocca chiusa

He made up a bed for her on the huge shelf that sat in the hood of the van over the driver's cab. Then he hopped out of the van, got into his swag and fell asleep under the stars as quickly as any soldier would. He had faced worse things than her confusion. When she started questioning him, he had convinced himself that it was best to confess in order to save the situation. That was one of the scenarios that they had game-planned in Canberra before he left. As he fell asleep, however, he had no idea of what she would do tomorrow. He hoped like hell her curiosity would keep everything on track.

The next day they drove in silence. Things were awkward – like a couple who had decided to break up – but who still had to finish the road trip. Now when she saw strange shapes by the side of the road – she knew they'd turn into buffaloes... Again, he parked off road that afternoon, again he set up the camp stove again the sun set. But this time the last of the kangaroo steaks really did confirm that she hated kangaroo. The wine had become merely a beverage and the conversation dull, as they two of them kept their thoughts strictly to themselves. She'd been trying her mobile phone all day. There was no signal.

As the sun's last light coincided again with the end of their meal, she asked him: "Should we blame Pandora for opening the jar? Or the idiot gods for putting all the world's evils into the jar in the first place?"

He had no answer. It was a game he didn't want to play.

On their second night under the stars, he prepared her bed in the van exactly as he had the night before. As they took turns brushing their teeth at the small sink. They didn't really speak. This second night was as quiet as the first, and the night breeze on her cheek was still cool. Annabelle climbed up to her bed above the cab for the last time. Her mind was buzzing with thoughts. She looked at her phone one last time – still no reception. No chance to call home, to call anyone.

But tonight she was more agitated, and she couldn't ask him for reassurance. So out of her backpack she took a pen, a small notebook, and used the light on her phone to write. She wrote down everything she could remember about their conversation. She self-edited. The sex wasn't mentioned, but everything else went in. Then she switched off the small light and just lay there in the dark thinking. Beyond a small vent in the side of the van, she could see that it was dark for hundreds of miles and there were dim white stars on the horizon... She'd been angry all day. She'd regretted telling him about Stella. It was obvious now that the first thing he would do when he got to the base would be to make a report about the boxes of letters. The feds would seize them. Stella would be shouting at them to "fuck off." But still, they'd find them now. Once this was done, they would completely control the narrative.

"Sorry Stella" she whispered quietly to her friend back in Sydney.

Annabelle put her light back on, ripped the pages she'd been writing out of her notebook, folded them into a wad and pressed them behind one of the metal struts that held up the canopy over her head. It was a small gesture of defiance. She did it more out of hope than to be practical. It was a tiny act to try to get her own story out – somehow – no matter what happened tomorrow. She imagined that someone finding the notes one day. She switched the light off again and tried to sleep.

She was weary but for a long time she couldn't sleep - she was too disturbed. She didn't know what *their* narrative was. She didn't like the fact that what seemed to be her story was theirs and she was just a character in it. She knew that she would have a starring role in letting out the truth – but now she knew that the big reveal was part of *their* plan not hers. And how could she trust Black Veil now? How could she know what to think?

And why her? They could have used anyone to do this. Maybe the only way to fuck it all up was to turn back now and refuse to play the role she'd been given. She wondered for a while if he'd left the keys in the ignition. She could just sneak into the cab and speed off right now...

But if she did turn back – the story would slip through her fingers. If it was indeed a story she could make her own...

In her stomach she felt the kangaroo steaks screaming at her – *don't go! For fuck's sake! It's a trap...keep away...trust your guts*. But it was also about then that she fell asleep confused and exhausted. As she fell into sleep, her gut instinct hoped that she would remember, in the morning, that she needed to flee.

CHAPTER 7

The Last Day on Earth

The next morning, she heard him moving about. When she climbed down from her sleeping perch, she found he had packed everything – well almost – like yesterday morning there were bacon and eggs slowly frying on the camp stove. He kept an eye on the pan as he rolled up his swag. After she had brushed her teeth and hair, he handed her a plate full of food. They sat and ate, again, in silence.

After swallowing her last mouthful of egg, she said to him, "I should probably get back to Canberra. I can't walk into a trap like this – I don't know what's going to happen. I'll just forget everything you told me and try to get on with my life."

She thought she saw him smirk for a millisecond and then he nodded seriously. "I'll get you home safe. The easiest way to do this is to drive you to the base – there's a plane landing today that will be waiting to take me back – you can come too. I'm sure someone will want to debrief you before they let you return to reality. You might have to sign the Official Secrets Act..."

She looked at him. "Did you smirk just then?"

He stared at her sincerely. "Yeah, I did – I just can't imagine you turning down a story like this. But if that's what you want... we can make it happen."

"It's not a story, it's a trap" she mumbled getting up.

He finished his eggs before adding: "We've shared a lot over the years, Annabelle. If you want to go home, I'll make sure you get back safely." He stood and washed up the last few things while the cooker cooled off. Eventually, he packed that up too and closed the back door of the ute and invited her to get back into the cab.

She wanted to believe him, but she also knew she had to doubt everything, so she was reluctant to move. "How can you be so *certain* that either of us will be safe?"

He looked down at the ground in disbelief. "Do you realise the importance of what we know? Do you understand that the rest of the world, the diplomatic communities of the planet, and the entire country – none of them knows what we know? The international spy community knows nothing – do you know what power that gives us? If we decided that the best way to get back to Canberra was riding in our own fleet of Apache helicopters then the Chief of Defence would have them on the horizon before I'd put the phone down." He stepped closer to her and put his hand on her arm, "We're safe, ok? If we go back to Canberra, we will remain safe. We have no proof; we just need to shut up. All will be well."

She did not trust him when he said they would be safe. She did not trust him when he said she should get the story. She did not trust him when he said they should leave the story and just go back home. She was starting to feel very dumb. She was feeling that instinct was all she had.

They drove through the morning. On the stereo, Robert Smith was singing about 'in-between days'. She got the shits with the music and pressed the eject button. The CD popped partly out of the player and rested there. The rest of the trip was nothing but the noise of the wheels on a dusty, empty, tarmac road.

After about four hours, a huge orange radar tower appeared on the distant horizon. "That's the base," he mumbled. After a while she could see that next to the tower were a number of barracks and aircraft hangars. The base didn't look too sophisticated. A little while longer, houses started appearing along the roadside and Black Veil brought the ute to an amble. Kids were running about chasing and screaming at each other. Suddenly on the right was a large wire mesh fence and the sewerage works behind it.

"Is that the launch site?" she asked.

"Yep – one of them," he mumbled.

She looked at the six huge, galvanised water tanks behind the works. It was hard to believe what he had said – but the site was a strange one. Four of those huge tanks covered underground nuclear silos. It was easy to see how that could be. A settlement this small didn't really need all that water capacity, did it? She wondered why no one had questioned the size of the plant...

A few blocks down the road, a pub appeared. He turned the ute into the sandy car park at the front. "You'll need to stay here for a bit while I go over to the base and call Canberra. I'll tell them it's 'no deal' and that you'll be coming back with me. You can get some lunch and I'll get some instructions, ok?"

She got out of the cab and heard him drive off behind her. She went in and asked the barman for a beer and a menu. She took these to a table in the corner of what was in fact a large metal shed – one with air-conditioners welded into the sheet metal walls every two meters or so. She started to read the menu, but as she passed her eyes over the unappealing list of fried food and hamburgers, a very strange feeling came over her. She looked up and saw 15 men in stubbies and blue singlets hanging off the bar and staring at her. She looked at them for a while, then she began staring them down – but their eyes refused to blink.

It was so intense she started smiling then shouted defiantly at them. "What's wrong boys? Do they not have women in these parts?"

One of the old men on a stool at the bar raised his hand towards her like he was death itself and tried to restrain himself as he shouted out "You're fucking Annabelle Jones!"

She could only say "Yes, yes I am."

It turned out that the whole town was addicted to *Sunday Review* – a political analysis program that aired on Sunday mornings. Annabelle sometimes appeared on it. "Fucking Annabelle Jones! God Damn!" she heard someone shout. One guy was on his mobile saying "...no, really it's her! She just admitted it. Get ya arse over here." They crowded around her. They wanted selfies with her, they got her to sign beer coasters, they wanted to ask how she got on with the grumpy old host of *Sunday Review*, they asked about the politicians she'd met. They all knew about the police raids she had had to put up with, and they shared with her their anger and sympathy. And every now and then she'd hear someone else shouting out "Fucking Annabelle Jones! Can you believe it?"

The old guy who first spoke got off his stool and came over to her table to shake her hand saying "No, really – we love that show – we all get down here on Sunday mornings and watch it. We don't have a church in town, see – so your show is the next best thing!"

"That makes you..." said one young guy, "...at least a saint."

"The goddess of truth," she heard another voice say.

She found herself blushing at the attention. "So, you guys like good journalism, hey?" She dared to ask.

"Hell yeah!" One guy shouted. "Them politicians are full of bullshit and we need to know by how much bullshit they are full of it – and you tell us!" The whole room burst into laughter at this.

Annabelle was suddenly profoundly touched. These men weren't staring at her because she was a woman, but because she was exactly who they thought she was.

"Now tell me dear," said the old man "...what on earth brings ya up here?"

Annabelle went straight to her cover story – "Oh, me and a friend thought we'd drive from Darwin to Broome – just to see what it's like up here – hey... and then I get to meet you guys as well! That's a bloody treat..."

"Where's your friend?" Someone asked and the room fell silent waiting for the answer.

She had to announce to them all that "He's gone to get petrol – he'll be back soon – we're going to get some lunch and get back on the road – but it's been brilliant meeting you all."

The old man put up his hands and the crowd of excited men fell in behind him. "Now Ms. Jones, we're very sorry to have disturbed you.

We are great respecters of personal privacy up here, but I hope you understand how excited we all were to see you walking into our humble pub – ya shining presence has made our week. Our year! We love your show, we love what you do...I'm sure I speak for us all when I say - please, keep doing it!"

Someone shouted, "Yeah, keep the bastards honest!"

The old man carried on, "We're honoured that you have passed through our little world... Now you better get yourself some lunch, because all of us are going over to a basketball game at the base. And I mean everyone. There'll be no one left. It starts in about an hour – so this whole place is about to become a ghost town. Please enjoy the beer and have a good feed – and don't worry about the bill – have what ya like – it's on us!"

At that there was a collective cheer and she stood up and thanked them again. She autographed a few more beer coasters, starred in a few more joint selfies, and then sat back down to study the menu. She decided to order something for Black Veil, got him a beer as well and waited for him to return.

When he walked in, he saw that everyone was looking him over. Approvingly it seemed – the old man stuck up his thumb as if to say, "that's indeed a fine frame of a 'friend' you got yourself there Ms. Jones."

"What the fuck's going on in here?" he asked in a whisper.

"Apparently the only thing they do up here is watch *Sunday Review.*"

He chuckled, "Oh – were you recognised by your fans, were you?"

She smiled even more "No, I was *mobbed...*" She pushed a plate towards him. "The food and the beer are on them – but they have advised us to eat quick because, wouldn't you know it, they're all going to the basketball game over at the base and any minute now this place will be closing."

"Ah," he nodded. Then, under his breath said "I put a call through to the Chief. I didn't speak to him, but he'll work out soon enough that something's up and I should get a call back when we get to the base."

They ate their lunch. As they did so, the place emptied. After eating, they walked out the front door and lingered on the veranda. The barman swiftly locked up behind them and headed for his ute, stuffing a huge bunch of keys in his pocket as he fled. They looked around. The whole town had been abandoned.

He wasn't sure what to do next. "Nothing's going to happen – not until after this bloody game – so do you want to go and watch it? I don't think there's anything else to do..."

Annabelle was still getting over her experience in the pub. "You know what... why don't you take me to this health clinic first – at least then I can say I've *seen* the building."

"You sure?" He asked quizzically...

"Yep, let's go..."

They got in the ute and drove off down the street.

CHAPTER 8

Lasciate ogne speranza, voi ch'intrate

He pulled up and she got out. It was exactly as he had described it. A wooden sign out the front read "United States, Commonwealth of Australia: Joint Health Clinic." The front of the brick building was indeed full of windows – but just like the rest of the town, the whole place seemed freshly abandoned.

"Do you want to see 'the door'?" he asked her temptingly. She nodded, and the two of them walked around the back. The rear wall of the clinic had been covered in graffiti by the local kids, but there, right in the middle of the wall, was a metal door. It looked like a fire exit no one ever used. He put his key in the lock and after an amount of twisting and jiggling, the door opened outwards. The two of them stared downwards as a flight of stairs on the other side of the threshold descended into the darkness. The earthy smell of cold, damp concrete slapped them in the face.

She pointed at the lock. "How were you going to explain to me that you had a key?"

He gave a small laugh, "They really take that hiding in plain sight philosophy seriously – this is just a standard military lock. We use on a lot of buildings – storerooms, offices – it's only the *next* door that's impenetrable... down there in the darkness somewhere. That's the security check. That door's got a biometric lock on it. You could never have got through it. But they chocked it open..."

"And with me in mind hey?" She didn't smile.

"After the door with a biometric lock, there's only one other door. The final door is a steel blast door, it only closes when the control room is online. So if it is open as well, then there's nothing between us and the control room except this vertiginous stairway – your stairway to hell as it were..."

She stared into the darkness. "Would you go down?" she asked.

"Fuck no."

"Why not?"

"Because I have strict orders not to."

She smiled. "You didn't obey orders when you leaked to me – or were you ordered to leak?"

"Oh, for fuck's sake! Don't underestimate the sophistication of my training – they also teach us about the moral duties of the soldier and the ethical need to remain critical of commands that breach international conventions. None of us are unthinking robots."

"So..." She said daring him to prove he could be on her side again, "...come down with me."

"No way" he said, standing there still holding the door open, "...if you want to know what I genuinely think here it is." He took a solid breath "– I think you're perfectly correct. It's a fucking trap. You are indeed being set up. The Americans have gone to a hell of a lot of trouble to get you up here, and they're risking their cosy relations with the people of this country, and giving away one of their greatest national secrets, *and* they are risking an international scandal by letting you go down these stairs... and, just like you, I can't work out why the fuck they are doing this. So, as one human to another Annabelle, and here is my final word - I think the last thing you should do is go down these fucking stairs...Just don't do it."

She peered down the stairs and into the darkness. "Agreed" she said stepping back.

After they both looked down the staircase one last time, he closed the door and made sure it was locked. Then they walked back to the ute and a sense of finality came over them both.

But when she put her hand on the handle of the passenger-side door, a profound emotion struck her. She realised she should trust no one. "Are you using reverse psychology on me?" she asked as she opened the ute door and looked at him as he got into the driver's seat.

He looked across the bench seat of the ute. "You've got to be joking – this has got to be one story that's not worth the risk. Fuck'n just get in and we'll go watch the game, and then we can get a flight home. Forget about it. Get in."

She grabbed her backpack from behind her seat and started putting it on. "Fuck you, Mr Boy Scout... I'm not buying your 'genuine confession' garbage..." Now she was overtaken by a definite bloody-mindedness – "Unlock the door. I'm going down...."

He looked at her in astonishment. "You can't do that... You shouldn't do that..."

She walked back to the clinic and tugged on the handle of the door. "Come on, unlock it – I'm a journalist, aren't I? I'm an angel of truth! And leave the ute for me – I might make it back out. If I do - I'll need it."

He was torn. If he unlocked the door, he was doing exactly what he was ordered to do. If he refused, he was saving her from the unimaginable. He just stood there, lost.

"Open the fucking door," she shouted at him.

He did so reluctantly. He hoped the darkness and the descent would change her mind. As she pushed past him, she looked up into his eyes. "Here's looking at you, kiddo," she said and winked. It was all so sudden.

The last he saw of her was her back and shoulders flexing and the darkness of her bag as she descended the stairs, and then there was her hand on the rail which was illuminated by a spot of the midday sun above him, and then there was her form getting smaller and smaller as the subterranean darkness enveloped her. When he could see her no more, he realised there was nothing more he could do. He flipped the catch on the door lock and pushed it closed from the outside. He made sure it was locked for the second time and he leaned against it, wondering... He wondered if he would hear her knock on the other side. He hoped she would return. After a while he realised she wouldn't.

When the crowds started returning from the game and repopulating the township, he put the key of the ute in the glovebox under the logbooks – exactly where he knew she'd look for them – and he walked back over to the base. The staff asked no questions and showed him to the officers' mess hall.

Every now and then he heard American voices in the corridor outside the room – all they talked about was the game. The excitement of the match was still bouncing around the base.

The Australians had won.

At 17:50 local time, one of the RAAF's Special Purpose Boeings landed at the base. He watched as about 15 people got off in the distance. He couldn't tell who they were. The sun was behind them, and he couldn't even see what they were wearing – civilian clothes or military uniforms? He wasn't sure. As he walked out onto the tarmac himself, three RAAF helicopters landed. As the aircrew showed him to his seat, he watched through one of the Boeing's windows as more personnel moved away from the choppers. They were moving casually. Nothing seemed wrong. The plane taxied smoothly, and by 6.10PM he was in the air. The plane turned for Canberra. Only then did he realise he was the only passenger.

With no one about, Black Veil felt a mass of emotions pass through him. He cried quietly to himself as the plane charged southwards through the evening.

He had told her what he really thought – that it was a trap... but of all the times she had believed him, the one time she should have, she didn't. He was numb. He'd failed to hide his true motivations, and yet he had still succeeded in getting her into that damned room. Ironically, and despite his best intensions, he'd followed out his orders with precision and he had little idea of how he had done it.

As his plane passed out of Western Australian airspace, he felt more like an executioner than a soldier. He had no idea what would happen next – to himself, or to Annabelle Jones.

He understood, too, that it was his job to withstand the mystery he had just confronted and ask no further questions. But he felt he was failing in this as well. Back in Canberra he'd be grilled, he'd file a report, and that was it. Maybe he'd learn something about her fate in tomorrow's newspaper.

His career was now over. As he hid in his seat, he realised he was already retired. Most people he knew thought of him as an upstanding patriot. But what would they think when they learned he'd lured a civilian into a military installation and left her there for dead?

Whether she was safe or not, he knew he'd never see her again.

As he went over and over his feeling of guilt and unease, the plane flew on.

II

El Presidente

CHAPTER 9

Fly Trap

At the bottom of the stairs, she found a hallway turning to the right. She made her way along it. Everything down here was surgically clean. But the smell of dank concrete never gave up assaulting her senses. From the start of the hallway, she could see light up ahead. Annabelle could make out the shape of a door in the far distance. It emitted a quiet but constant beep that drew her towards it. She assumed this must be the biometric security door. She carried on, thankful that there were no more stairs – the staircase she had just come down seemed to go forever. As she walked on down the hall, she felt she was in the bowels of the earth. She felt she was 20 metres underground, maybe more. As she moved towards the open door ahead of her, she could see that a small amount of light was coming from another stairwell to her right. She thought that these must be the stairs that descended from inside the clinic – the ones that monitoring staff used to come and go without observation. The corridor she was now walking along and the stairwell from the clinic met at a small space before the door with the biometric lock. Keypads on the wall near it were flicking green. It was exactly as Black Veil had explained it. The door itself was chocked open with a wedge of ancient, splintered wood. She smiled at this, because she didn't know what else to do. The most secret place in the country had its security door chocked open like it was a fire door that sneaky employees had disabled so that they could get outside for a cigarette.

Once a strange laugh escaped her lungs at this whole situation, she found that she was overcome with dread. The door had been chocked open specifically so she could pass through, this was all being done for her. She was the fly, and the trap was just ahead. Or she was indeed Pandora and the box had been pre-unlocked, the lid jiggled almost to being open. Everything had been done to make sure her tiny little force of curiosity would lift the lid off all this quite completely – even though she just wanted the merest peek inside. No doubt all the evils of the world were about to hatch out.

After walking through the chocked-open security door, Annabelle could see down another gloomy corridor ahead. Another doorway beckoned her. She assumed it was the blast door.

As she approached it, she could see that the frame of this last door was metres thick. On the other side, small indicator lights and the cool green glow of sleeping monitor screens beckoned her. The closer she got, the cooler and more breathable the air became. The space ahead seemed welcoming and familiar – like a newspaper office late at night. She paused for a while, trying to see into the room, but the thickness of the walls and the narrowness of the door made that difficult. Then at last, she walked in and looked about. She saw the three chairs, the control panel, the far door that led to the toilet... It was an eerie place because she really did expect uniformed officers to be sitting in their chairs, waiting to press buttons, their faces welded to screens with such intent that they couldn't turn their heads around to look at her as she watched them.

She got out her camera. Then she sat wondering. But as she turned around and around in her chair taking photos she kept asking why, of all people, she had been the chosen one, the one who got to be here. As she ran this question over and over in her mind, she did not see the massive vault door slowly and silently begin to move.

By the time she did notice it, there was no room for her to slip past it and get back outside. Only when she heard the shooting of the five stainless steel bolts into the door frame did she realise that Black Veil was right.

It was a trap.

Now, she was caught.

CHAPTER 10

Michael Macintosh Foot

The light changed in the room – mainly because the huge screen in front of her was powering up. The room itself had a high ceiling, so this main screen, sitting as it was on top of the long console, was still about 2 metres high. If she sat on a chair at the console and looked up for too long, it would have pinched all of her neck muscles. So, she stood instead, and waited for the image to resolve itself as electricity passed through it. While this was happening, she walked over and put her hand on the vault door. It was as solid as it seemed to be. Perfectly immovable. There was no way to open it from the inside. She ran her eyes all the way along the console to see if there was a door-release button. Nothing.

The screen came on to show an upholstered wooden dining chair. Its upholstery was a dark blue – as was the carpet. The screen *looked* American – in the way that American television systems are of lower quality than British and Australian systems. The walls behind the chair were white. She could hear voices mumbling – as if one voice was briefing another – but away from the microphone. The other voice was just going "yep, yep, got it, yep..." Annabelle couldn't take her eyes of the screen while all this was happening. The build-up was intense – it was as if the fucking President of the United States himself was about to sit down in the chair and start talking to her...

Then a slim man in a black tuxedo, white shirt with formal wingtips as a collar and a white bowtie walked from where the camera was and literally jumped into the chair – like he was some kind of acrobat on speed. As he did this, he was fixing a discrete headset and microphone to his head. It wasn't sitting correctly behind his neck – a woman in a naval uniform stepped into sight and re-adjusted it, then she stepped out of the frame just as quickly. It was only then that Annabelle got to see the face of the thin, nimble man.

She was shocked. "Jesus fucking Christ!" she mumbled under her breath when she saw who it was.

"Is that a theological statement, Ms Jones? Or just a regular old Aussie expletive?"

Sorry, "I was just thinking – wouldn't be funny if the President of the United States sat down, and then..."

"And here I am," he said still adjusting himself and the headset.

Annabelle shook her head "Which means this is fucking serious."

He nodded. "Ah yes, it is serious and yet I'm not exactly in the perfect state to deal with the seriousness of what we have to discuss.... Excuse me if I come across as a bit flippant, Ms Jones. That would be because it is midnight here in Washington, and I've just come from a state reception for the kings of Morocco and Jordan – and the new Sultan of Brunei. Who, I am happy to report, is not as rampantly homophobic as his predecessor..."

There was a pause as he looked her over. "So..." he said, trying to seem welcoming "I hope you are well...."

She genuinely didn't know what to say.

"So..." he repeated and smiled warmly at her while fixing his coat. He seemed the kind of man who smiled a lot. He took a pen out of his jacket pocket and clicked the button on its top – not to write anything but just to hear the reassuring click. He looked off screen again – maybe confirming that the sound was working. Once he could feel that everything was in place by another random click of his pen he said: "You don't mind if I ask that this conversation be off the record? A background briefing. You're *so good* at keeping the anonymity of your sources, I hope that I can be counted amongst them?" *Click, click* went the pen.

She looked warily at him. "That's a big ask."

"Well, I mean I hope the existence of the room itself is a big enough story for you – no need to mention also that the President of the United States appeared on screen to give you the cook's tour? And to be frank – and I would like to be frank with you... We have some big problems to discuss – and I would like to tell you what is on my mind without fear that you will expose every nasty little corner of my cranium..."

Annabelle was just slightly charmed by his smile "O.K. – let's do this off the record – you have my word as a journalist."

"Thank you, Ms. Jones. I trust your sense of professional integrity." said the man with utmost sincerity and clicked his pen again. "Now – do you know who I've been thinking of lately?"

It was an impossible question "I have no idea," she said.

"Mr Michael Macintosh Foot," he replied.

Annabelle didn't know what he meant. "Who?"

The president laughed at her confusion. "Have a seat Ms. Jones – it helps if you put one of the chairs against the far wall – then your neck will be a little more relaxed looking up at the screen..."

He waited while Annabelle readjusted the chair and sat.

"Michael Foot – Surely you've heard of him?" The president asked again.

She was still getting over the fact that he knew her name - but she tried to answer his question. "Do you mean the British Labour opposition leader – back when Margaret Thatcher was PM?"

"Exactly! Perfect!" he chortled down the screen. "No one in Washington has ever heard of the man – thank God you Australians keep up with your British political history..." Then he pointed off camera no doubt to the people standing around the room behind the camera. "Little do they know that I wrote my Master's thesis on Michael Foot – Political Science degree at Cambridge. The man fascinated me, always has. Very left-wing, strange grooming habits, sort of the political grandfather of Jeremy Corbyn... who, of course, shared the same fate... You see... Foot had this raft of immovable, uncompromisable political standards that meant he never had any hope of being elected. But by God, he stood by those convictions...Then spent his years in the wilderness of opposition. He wrote a raft of books about Labour history. His biography of Aneurin Bevan, for example, is one of the most masterful works on political... well, political *desire* let's say... the unwavering political urge for social change..."

'Who?" Annabelle was still getting her head around precisely who it was she was speaking to.

"Aneurin Bevan – another long-lost warrior for what is politically astute. I've always been in love with British politics. Still am – and particularly that old army of left-wingers that have hung off the British Labour party like 'flies on a sheep's arsehole...' as you Australians would say – Tony Benn, Neil Kinnock – politicians who'd never let the possibility of electoral victory interfere with their convictions. Every one of them a Bernie Sanders... long before Bernie was ever heard of... I mean some people in Washington have heard of Neil Kinnock. Oh, you bet you they have!" Here at last he seemed to take a breath and slow down some.

"Did you know Neil Kinnock, leader of the British Labour Party from 1983 to 1992 – did you know he wrote nearly all of Joe Biden's presidential campaign speeches? Problem was - no one asked Kinnock if that was ok, and Biden, the senile old bastard, told no one what he'd done – until we worked it out for ourselves... stupid old plagiarist... still, he made it to the White House... Biden's mouth, Kinnock's words – tempered, of course, for an American *sensibility*...."

Annabelle was still unsure what to make of this on-rush of words... but it was clear that the man was good at channelling his thoughts through history. "You're an erudite bastard aren't you..."

"Yeah... just look at me." The President said with a subtle Southern tinge to his accent. "Rambling on about old lefties... see, this is how my mind really works, Ms Jones – full of enthusiasms – and only when I'm speaking off record can I really let people know what I'm thinking... mainly I have to "folksy it up" for local consumption.... but this is who

I've been thinking about... Michael Foot, Neil Kinnock, Corbyn, even Sanders – they were right, they saw the system for what it was, and they wanted to radically change it – and for a time they won a certain enthusiasm amongst the people with their reasoning... But they were wrong in how they judged the electorate's desires..." He shook his head a little. "They haunt me... with their tragic auras"

"See, there's a profound sadness to each of their tales... don't you think? Being both correct and also totally unelectable..."

Annabelle was growing angry that he had turned her into some kind of sounding board for his cascade of words. "I don't know, I wasn't alive back then..."

He smiled. "Neither was I – but I think that's what most fascinates me – is the great game...you know... how do you take something like British political discourse and transfer it to Washington? I mean Biden and his plagiarism showed that you could do it – *House of Cards* – who would have thought that a drama written by Baron Dobbs of Wylye – created to exact maximum revenge against his former boss—the dreaded Maggie T.—could have been so successfully transplanted here? Well, until Kevin Spacey *literally* fucked it all up – as you know... Wow. Hashtag "me too"! So, anyway, I have been thinking about all this, because I have been wondering how do political ideas transfer around the Anglosphere? And how can I explain to you what the nexus of our problem is tonight. How can I get you to empathise about a particularly *American* political situation and get you to understand it from your *Canberra*-dweller's journalistic intuition? I think I've worked out how to do it – I hope you don't mind if I bend your ear for an hour or so to see if it works? and beyond my present flippancy – well, I think I am coming across a bit flippant – maybe because it is such a horrible conundrum that I want to share with you... and I really..." he paused and smiled at her, "I really want your dispassionate feedback..."

Annabelle was reeling from the torrent of words coming out of the thin, eager man's mouth, but finally she got to answer him. "Well, I don't think I can go anywhere anyway – so why don't you just keep talking... Although I would like to know if you going to let me out when you're done?"

He smiled. "Of course, I'll let you out – or I'll let someone out..." He suddenly stopped talking – realising he may have said too much.

"What do you mean?" She demanded.

"Well, I'm not sure you'll be the same person when you exit. So perhaps in one sense the 'you' who is existentially *you* at the present moment may never leave the room... and only the 'you' who will become 'you' over the next few hours will be the 'you' that gets released into the wild, as it were... when the door is unlocked..."

"That's fucking ominous," she said half sarcastically.

"Sorry, in college I was a big fan of Heraclitus – you know 'no man steps into the same river twice – it's not the same river, he's not the same man...' that sort of thing – I suppose I'm letting my own feelings infect my talk. But I want to give you a sense of what it is like to be president. Because this is how this office works – you enter as one person, you get beaten about the head by the Leader of the Senate and the House Majority Leader for 4 or 8 years and then you come out of office another person entirely. Despite this, you have to spend the whole time pretending you are the same soul – when you certainly aren't... or can't be... the job changes you – knowing you have some ultimate responsibility for rooms like the room you're in – that changes you – really changes you..."

"You have my sympathies" she said dryly.

"All I can say is relax – I'm from the South! It's in my genes to be able to put you at ease."

"Really reassuring," she confirmed.

He jumped up in his chair and clicked his pen again, "Ah! That was Australian sarcasm you just laid on me then! I'm collecting examples – I'll put that one in my scrapbook... almost missed it."

She was not impressed by what seemed to be his unceasing enthusiasm. "Listen – tell me one thing before you start – why me?"

He sat back down again. "Because like Michael Foot, Ms Jones, you're an old leftie underneath it all – aren't you? Beneath all that journalistic impartiality, you've got a social conscience. And, as a journalist, you haven't had to make any kind of journey towards compromising that political outlook of yours – which is perfect! As we speak, your old, left, convictions remain intact prehistorically there under all the new world sophistication and analysis you've loaded on top of it... And I really need to see where that will lead us this evening – of course, I mean for you, this afternoon."

He got up and turned the chair around – Kristine Keeler style and sat down again leaning closer into the camera. "You know... this is the irony. I never asked for this. When I was in my 20s, I was trying to make myself the world's greatest political scientist. That's all I wanted to be – tenure track, middle-class, scholar and analysist. I wanted to be more like you than me... I studied political systems from all over the world. I dug up old political ideas like Indiana Jones unearths Arks of the Covenant. I would tell my friends about how you could adapt these ideas for this present crisis or that present crisis. You know what they said to me? 'Sheet man, you should go into office' or 'Jeff, you got all the ideas – when you gunna run?' or 'There's this position coming up – we're gunna nominate you whether you want it or not.' Hell – I became a politician before I'd even committed myself to a cause. Which helped my popularity - I was a million causes to a million different people – not because I was a spineless two-faced motherfucking political jerkoff – but because I had dedicated my life to studying *all* the possible political solutions and – when a problem arose – I was able to select the best one *despite* party ideology. I was the darling of the bipartisan set. And, of course, I was really lucky – I came across to the voters as intelligent, urbane, and sophisticated – which is exactly what the country desperately wanted after the ghost of Donald Trump and the threat of Don Junior running.... And let's be honest – Kamala Harris scared the shit out of people – which is why, after Biden dropped dead from old age, the Democrats found a nice, relatively young white guy to take the nomination." He turned his face side on to the camera. "...and a little bit Kennedy too – don't you think? On my right side...? And I rode all those tensions and fears to the White Ho–se, Ms. Jones, and here I am – a child of fortune whose academic career, I realised when standing up on the Capitol taking the oath of office, had been horribly, horribly misdirected, perhaps even misspent completely. But through all this, I realised that being in politics meant that the moment I entered the arena, I had to stand for something. I had to retrofit myself to an ideology. I had to fight for the right solutions within a wider matrix of personal beliefs."

He paused. "It's something a journalist never has to do... am I correct? For you politics can remain a delightful game that others play..."

Annabelle was still not in a mood to humour him and stayed quiet. It didn't stop him from going on.

"In fact, as a journalist, you can convince yourself that you shouldn't commit to a political conviction – that you should just worry about reporting on other people's politics and leave your own political opinions locked in the safe at home. But this afternoon, I'm going to ask you to try to commit to something – I want to see *if* you can, and then *how* you can. I want some reflections on my own thoughts because these are indeed troubling times we are in - aren't they?"

"Commit to what?" she said, a little annoyed and trying to shut him up.

"Well, you'll have to indulge me – I'll explain as we go – I mean as the leader of the free world – surely, I can bend an Australian journalist's ear for a little while and get to see how she thinks?"

Annabelle saw an opportunity. "So, you want me to take part in your problematic? Happy to do so, but you have to answer some questions for me first."

"Sure," he said staring straight at her from the screen. "Fire away."

CHAPTER 11

From Baghdad

"My questions are principally about the room that I am sitting in."

"Sure," he said again.

"No bullshit?"

He smiled with the same inane enthusiasm he'd been deploying from the start. "I want your truthful reactions later on – so you can have my truthful reactions now."

"Ok – so this room I am in – is it a nuclear missile control room?"

"It is."

"So, you can fire nuclear weapons from here?"

"I would consult with the Australian Prime Minister before I did anything – as a matter of courtesy..." He started clicking his pen again.

"So, have all the Australian Prime Ministers known about this?"

"I was still in elementary school when construction on these missile sites started, Ms. Jones. John Howard was the one who invited American troops to settle in northern Australia. The Pentagon commenced the installations about then – early 2007, I think. So, in many respects, this meeting of ours has nothing to do with us – but was set up long ago in the prehistoric times of Howard and George "dubya." We're simply the fruits of their strange and ingratiating friendship.

"Then, of course, it took decades to sneak the equipment in and get everything fully functional – all done under the cloak of absolute secrecy. The lengths that were gone to were exacting. Apparently, the US military was waiting for the right moment to brief Rudd, Gillard, Rudd, Abbott, and Trudball... sorry, *Turnbull*, about what we were doing – but they were so quickly in and out of office that our boys never really got the chance to explain what the project was all about. And then there was the touchy issue of the international treaty on medium-range missiles we'd signed with the Russians.... But then Trump fucked that all up – so, once the treaties with the Russians were trashed – it was easier to brief The Lodge. Every Australian Prime Minister since Morrison has been fully informed about the program – and they can see why and how we're doing it."

"Why *are* you doing it? I mean, the Australian people will be furious when they find out the Top End is hosting American nukes."

He raised both his hands in the air. "Well, the gig's up – you found us out and you're going to be a part of the process we use to tell the Australian people about what we've done. You'll make it easier for us to explain."

"How?"

He chuckled, "Well, for a start you've got such an engaging writing style..."

"That's bullshit!"

"Oh, don't be so down on yourself – you really are an engaging writer. In fact, it's the reason you're here... I read all your stuff about Australian war crimes in Afghanistan – your discussion of the insanity of keeping troops there really influenced my attitudes to foreign policy... I relied on you then, and now I want to rely on you again... If a little more informally."

"Thank you," Annabelle said, sincerely abashed. "But I'm not calling bullshit on my writing style, I'm calling bullshit on the idea that I'm up here for the news scoop of my career. Just then you didn't say I would break the news of this installation – but that I would 'play a part' in how *you* broke the news. This is not a scoop – except that I have been scooped up into your trap. The operative who brought me up here – I call him..."

"You call him Black Veil. We know that," the President interrupted. "His name is Henry Segal and he works in the Signals Directorate for the Australian Defence Force. He has a phenomenally high security clearance and he's been briefing you secretly for decades. We know. We know. We found out what he was doing last year, and we forced him to bring you up here under the pretence that you were about to break the story of a lifetime..."

The President then smiled reassuringly. "Let me convince you that this will be the case. Whatever that charming little traitor told you, whatever doubts he has instilled in you, I can say for certain that you *will* be breaking this story. That's why you are here. But there is some background to the reveal – and that's why I want to talk through my little problematic with you. Are you ready?"

"Sure" she said, trying to seem calm while her heart throbbed in her throat. She realised now that this man was going to tell her everything that she was desperate to know. He stood up, put his chair back the original way it was set up, sat, and folded his hands across his lap.

This was it. Annabelle realised she was about to discover the answers to every question that had been plaguing her.

CHAPTER 12

The Room

"But first, let me give you a tour around this exciting piece of technology that you are sitting inside. You've seen the toilet, I assume?"

She swung in her chair and looked behind her. "Yep – nothing remarkable there..."

"As you can see, there's nothing remarkable about this place at all – no underground dorms or mess rooms, no radiation filters in the aircon – that's because there are two kinds of control bunker. There are underground facilities like we have at Raven Rock here in the US – which is practically an underground city from where we can totally obliterate the entire Eurasian continent if we have to. The point of such a facility is to let the world know it is there. The deterrent aspect of nuclear arms needs to be fully on display. Deterrent facilities only work when foreign aggressors know that you have them... But what you're sitting in right now is designed to be so secret as to not exist. It is a stealth asset. A clandestine site. Built when we were under international obligations not to build sites like this... Its value is in its unexpectedness. And as you say – the Australian people will go 'ape shit' when they find out what we've done. But revealing the whereabouts of this facility fits into a strategic plan we have been developing for decades.

"And you're exactly right, Ms Jones – you are being used by us – but when you let the world know what you know, you'll still be a part of the news scoop of the century... I have not for one moment lost sight of the fact that you are one of Australia's leading journalists. That's why you're here."

She was still confused. "Why are you letting me tell them *now*...?"

"I'll get to that – but let us continue the tour..."

He looked off screen for a moment - "If I give an explicit order to make your control room live – look what happens." At that the President looked off screen again and said: "Can we make XV1 live please?"

Suddenly the dull lights and occasional blinking nodes on the console gave way to the brilliance of Manhattan Island on the Fourth of July.

"Whoa, what the fuck is happening?" Annabelle shouted at the screen. "Stop this, stop it!"

"Don't worry, everything is perfectly safe. You need special keys to activate the firing mechanisms, and you don't have those – so, you're perfectly safe. The military does this in training mode on a regular basis."

She looked directly into the screen. "It doesn't mean that I am not scared shitless..."

The President smiled again. "Hence the toilet behind you..."

"Funny," she said, unimpressed.

"So, if you go to the chair on your right, immediately in front of it is a large green button. It's green, so feel free to press it."

Warily, Annabelle reached out her hands and pushed the green button. The moment she did so, live video feeds of the three silo sites around the township came into view. One screen overlooked the sewerage facility she'd driven past before lunch, the other views looked down on large sheds in truck yards.

The President continued to explain: "The officer who sits in that chair is responsible for monitoring the missile sites – as you can see on the screens.

"Now go to the chair on the left. You can see that there's a green switch surrounded by a red border – give that a flick."

Warily, Annabelle moved to the other chair and flicked the button. As she did so, some additional lights came on.

"In this seat is the officer who confirms the verbal orders to fire..." He clicked his pen three times to emphasise the point.

Annabelle was a little confused. "Why verbal orders? Why don't you just launch the missiles by remote control from Washington?"

Here the President looked particularly eager to explain. "Well, whatever system we used to connect Washington and your control room there – it could be hacked. We can turn the controls on and off from here, we can make your control centre live and we can aim the missiles – but we can't fire them from the U.S. – there still needs to be a confirmed personal connection between here and there before anything can happen. And in this age of deep-fake videos – our service people are trained to establish beyond reasonable doubt that they are speaking to US command before they act. We use a series of verbal codes to ensure everyone is who they say they are. The firing of nuclear weapons is, what we call here in the White House, 'an undoable'."

"Fuck – an 'undoable'..." Annabelle mouthed the words in astonishment.

"Now..." said the President "If you go back to the middle chair – can you see there the three keyholes under clear plastic covers in the lower centre of the panel?" His pen clicked once more.

Annabelle lifted the plastic cover and searched with her fingers to better feel the black keyholes. Then as she reminded herself of what they were, she instantly recoiled her hand. "Fuck..."

"Yeah – what was it that Oppenheimer said: 'Now, I am become death, the destroyer of worlds.' What was that from? *The Mahabharata* I think."

Annabelle thought she should correct him and his godly arrogance. "No, it was the *Bhagavad Gita* – I'm sure of that."

He laughed. "Oh, you Australians – you really need to brush up on your Indian. *The Bhagavad Gita* is a chapter of the *Mahabharata...*"

"Oh." She said.

"Hmm," he replied.

"Anyway, those three keyholes are nothing. The power they can unleash was, when they were installed, considered quite considerable –

but now... as you know – the world is fully realising its own ability to destroy itself... In the age of ecological cataclysm, who needs to worry about nuclear annihilation? No need for an A-bomb when drought can make a much more sustainable wasteland than any A-bomb ever could!"

CHAPTER 13

Wayang Kulit

She sat down in the middle console chair and thanked God the keys were not sitting in their eyeless slots. Still, they *were* keyholes. She felt sick knowing that the action she used each day to open her front door was the same action it took to launch these flights of mass destruction...

"You Australians should brush up on your Indonesian as well..."

"Why is that?" she asked, unable to completely take her eyes off the keyholes in front of her.

At last, he put his pen back in his pocket and explained. "When I was in high school, I became fascinated with Wayang Kulit... it was part of a personal interest project I got involved in – I even spent a few months in Western Java as a teenager... got to see a lot of Wayang Kulit up close... it was a wonderful time of my life..."

Annabelle shrugged her shoulders.

"Javanese puppetry" Ms. Jones. He continued to explain "...and, being President, I can occasionally indulge my personal whims and obsessions – so, last week I invited the great Asep Sunadar to the White House. He's one of Indonesia's greatest *dalangs* – a puppet master. These men are both geniuses at story-telling and Olympic athletes in terms of the performances they are required to give. They sit up through the night without food, without sleep, without taking a break, and they tell the great stories of India – the *Ramayana*, the *Mahabharata* –

great heroes like Lord Arjuna and Lord Rama battling the monsters of chaos – all in puppet form. The hero's parts must be recited in Sanskrit – so these puppet masters have to be linguistic experts – but then there are clowns who hang around the heroes. They can speak whatever they like – Bahasa – English – and they are intensely funny. I couldn't stop laughing at Asep's performance last week, it really was a highlight of my presidency.... And it didn't end until dawn, but it was worth the sleep deprivation..."

Annabelle burrowed herself deeper into her chair. She was unsure where this was going.

"And then at the end, Asep came up to me and we thanked each other – he said it was already an honour to play the White House, so he was doubly honoured that I stayed up all night with him to watch the full story – he hadn't expected that... And I thanked him for an incredible performance. But I also asked him what I have asked many *dalangs*. I said – 'You're a good Indonesian?' 'Yes' he said, 'and you're a good Muslim too, aren't you?' And he replied 'yes, of course,' and so I asked, 'doesn't all this theatre, all these Hindu stories ride in the face of your beliefs?' And he replied – as many *dalangs* have replied to me before 'but that's what being Indonesian means!' Meaning, of course, that culture, faith, nationalism, and sense of self can be perfectly reconciled when you need them to be..."

Annabelle thought there was some moral to this tale that she needed to understand, but it wasn't clear so she asked, "why are you telling me this?"

"I suppose because what I am going to explain next isn't about Islam – it's about Indonesia..."

"And what is that?"

Over the screen, all the President's joviality seemed to drain away. "Did you know, Ms. Jones, that Jakarta is sinking; in fact it's almost sunk ..."

Annabelle was really unsure what this meant for shadow puppetry. "And...?"

Suddenly the President showed the very edge of his anger. "See, this is what I don't understand about your country – you have almost no interest in this do you? No interest in Javanese culture, nor the fact that for the last 30 years Jakarta, one of the great metropolises of your region, has been sinking. You just don't give a shit, do you? I don't know if you *people* should be saved..."

Annabelle thought she was about to get a dose of American Christianity and bit back. "Oh, this is about salvation, is it?"

The President looked warily down the camera at her: "What else is there to talk about in this world Ms. Jones? What else?"

The was a pause in which he gathered his resolve and carried on. "Let me give you a lesson in Indonesia as it is right now – an Indonesian 101. Jakarta is a mega-city, 10 million people if you count its population conservatively. It's also the most un-planned city on earth – it just sprawls south in a series of unending suburbs. Most of those suburbs don't have running water. So, the locals dig wells. And they drink from these wells. And as they slake their thirst, they have drunk dry the aquifer under the city. The more they drink, the more the city falls below sea level. It is ten times more dramatic than Venice...

"Of course, the government planned to move the entire city to the island of Borneo. 'Nusantara' they were calling it, but it never really happened. Corruption, slow planning, Covid.... But in Jakarta – there was no great crunch, no great collapse just a constant, unstoppable sinking..." He sighed at the thought of it.

"Of course, they built sea walls – but no one can stop the sea in the end. And the more the wells emptied, the more the city sank, the more the people moved out. People have been fleeing Jakarta by the tens of thousands every week for the last several months now. And this is what started the great move South. Hundreds of thousands of people moving south out of the capital and right across Java – pushing more and more people along with them. These crowds were then pushed further and faster by floods, the constant droughts that the tropic zones now suffer, breaks in the sea walls, and breaks in the food supply chain... In normal times, all of this might be manageable...but..."

Annabelle tried to fight back against his claim of her ignorance. "Droughts – crop failures in Java – yes, I've been reading about those..."

"Exactly...but the problem is *right across* Java. So now even more people are on the move. What hasn't been widely reported is what the Javanese are doing about it."

"What are they doing?" Annabelle started to feel that this was all going to a bad place.

"At first it was a call by some radical operatives in Jemaah Islamiyah to resettle those on the move... but then it got picked up also by the Nahdlatul Ulama of Indonesia – which is Indonesia's general clerical group – do you know how many members this group has?"

"No."

"About 45 million – roughly twice the population of Australia are members of this one social and religious organisation. It sees its task in this emergency to focus on humanitarian aid, to uphold Indonesian culture ...and their plan is now, well, maybe unstoppable..."

"What plan?" Annabelle asked with dread.

"To save as many Indonesians as they can by moving them south – away from Jakarta, and away from drought-stricken areas – away from areas where climate change is causing massive crop failures. The pressure on the southern coast has been incredible. Tens of thousands of people arrive there each hour seeking shelter. The government is atrophied, it can't respond. The Nahdlatul Ulama has taken charge and have realised that the only way they can save all these people is, as they say, *keluaran* – or exodus. And it is now I speak a word that all Australians have been trained in their very heart of hearts to slaver over and to fear."

Annabelle was unimpressed. "What word?"

The President simply said, "boats."

"Boats?" Annabelle was indeed fearful. "You mean, they're coming here?"

"They have to move south – it is the only way anyone in an a-temperate climate will be able to guarantee their own survival. Java just happens to be the first – the sinking of Jakarta has pushed them to the front of the queue as it were... but very soon we will see massive population shifts out of the tropics and towards the poles in every part of the earth."

Now he had her attention. "So, how many boats?" She asked.

The President took a piece of paper from off screen as though someone handed it to him. "We've been counting them via satellite and drone footage. At the latest estimation we guess that just over 57,000 boats are being prepared – fishing skips, trawlers, river boats, pleasure boats, stolen navy dinghies, landing skips – all of them are being loaded with people."

"57,000 boats? Are you joking? And you said 'loaded?' – I hope you mean 'prepared'?"

"No, we've got clear evidence that people are now getting onto the boats. They are being loaded. It's their Operation Dynamo, it's their Dunkirk as it were. To get past Australian naval forces, they know they'll have to launch simultaneously. They estimate all you have up in your northern seas is a couple of nuclear submarines looking out for the Chinese fleet. They will be no match for the great flotilla that is coming at them. It is going to be perfectly synchronised. An Armada of hundreds and hundreds of thousands of helpless, unarmed, thirsty, hungry people will be setting out to reach the northern shores of Australia over the ensuing months – weather permitting."

Annabelle was beside herself. "This is bullshit."

The President shook his head. "No, no... it's a very clever plan by millions of desperate people to save themselves...and relocate their nation."

She almost wanted to exit her own skin. "How many people?"

"Well, some of these boats may only be able to carry 10, 20 people...but others – the very large fishing trawlers and inter-island ferries for example, they can carry thousands. We estimate on the first wave about half a million – and this is only the first wave.... These are the boats that you can't stop. And when they land off your coast, they will be turning back to bring more and more. This is not being done for profit. These are not the shady plans of people smugglers... These sailors are working for their nation's survival."

She was still trying to understand what was happening. "How many boats will make it here?"

"Well, the only figures we have to go on is Vietnam after 1975 – about 50% of those who set off made it to shore, the other half drowned..."

"That still means 250,000 will land."

"In the first wave. But remember, the boat operators will be returning again and again. They're relocating Java as a humanitarian crisis the likes of which we have not seen."

"Have you spoken with Canberra?"

"Yes, and we can see that there is no way to stop this."

Annabelle was incredulous – "but even if they land – they'll die in the deserts up here."

The President was calm in rebutting her statement. "The Indonesians are desperate, but they aren't stupid. They will head to Broome, Darwin, Townsville. This will cause a humanitarian crisis of unprecedented scope and while you Australians try to deal with the mass arrivals, certain Indonesian operatives have been tasked with establishing convoys of trucks and cars to take the refugees further south. They will probably hijack the Darwin-Adelaide Railway line. We suspect low-level military involvement in all this – unarmed but organised – and we have seen certain communiques, from the Nahdlatul Ulama and elsewhere. There will be absolutely no guns – no one will be armed. Their power will simply be in their desperation and their numbers. There will be no reason for Australians to open fire. This is meant to be seen by the world as a humanitarian crisis – not an invasion. But it is, of course, technically an invasion. An invasion by an army formed by the climate crises of our age. An unstoppable army of the hungry and the thirsty.

CHAPTER 14

Cauterisation

The President put the piece of paper he had been holding on the floor and looked into the camera with a seriousness he had not displayed until now. Out came his pen again from its pocket. He clicked it. "Over the last thirty-odd years a plan has been developed – using climate projections from NASA – to deal with the massive shifts in population that climate change will potentially encourage. It is one of many plans – but the plan I want to speak to you about is called "Project Cauterization." It's a desperate plan – and one we hoped we'd never have to use – but now it seems to be the only thing we can do, and, as the beautiful, uncommitted leftie that you are, I wanted to ask you about it... you know, as a member of the Australian general public... I want a comment from a thinker about human nature – a watcher, rather than, someone who is a committed participant in the boxing ring of politics..."

Annabelle was dizzied by where these facts were leading. She was standing in amongst all this confusion but found it hard to stay on her feet – "Cauterisation?" she asked.

"Yes, it involves the precise and surgical use of nuclear weapons to create radioactive wastelands in some regions of the world – wastelands that will then 'cauterise' population flows to enable enough of what is left of the world to survive. Cauterisation will enable some nations to carry on. For example – here in the United States we are facing something similar – a great surge of people heading up from the south. It may be that I will soon have to give the order to cauterise the Mexican border..."

His pen fired off a range of clicks to cover his shame at these words.

Annabelle couldn't believe what she was hearing. "You're going to nuke Mexico?"

"We may have to...Unlike Australia, we have all the ships, gunboats, and aircraft carriers we need to protect the US from any concerted attempt to land illegally on our southern coasts. But what we don't have is an army capable of stopping millions of unarmed Mexican, Central and South Americans who may try to cross into the United States."

"Why can't you protect your own border with the massive conventional forces you have?"

He was quick to explain. "Yes, yes... we do have an army *large* enough to *do* that, but the generals believe that we do not have the will to spend months shooting dead the millions of unarmed people who will be desperately throwing themselves across the line – as it were. They won't be coming in ones and twos – but will be driven by hunger and arriving in their tens of thousands... Military psychologists are warning us that troops will get serious kill fatigue from shooting dead so many unarmed civilians ... Whereas boats downing other boats is far less psychologically traumatising – and the Mexicans don't have the numbers of boats that the Indonesians do... "

The president looked dejected as he explained: "This is where cauterisation saves us."

"The plan is to surgically bomb northern Mexico to create a radioactive no-man's land across the border. Anyone who tries to cross dies of radiation sickness well before they get to that pathetic little wall that Donald Trump supposedly put up. In this way, North American civilization is saved, Central and South America get to go to hell in a handcart." He clicked his pen to underline the tragedy of it all.

Annabelle could feel her skin crawl. "That's the most heinous and disgusting thing I have ever heard – if that happens, there needs to be an immediate international humanitarian response."

The President was riled. "It's too late for that Annabelle. You know it is. It really is. How can we expect the world to respond when it's the majority that will be suffering? There's 130 million in Mexico, 60 million in Central America and another 600 million in South America – as the climate shifts some might be able to survive down in Tierra del Fuego, or Patagonia, but the rest are all going to need food and water when the food chains continue to collapse – and this is certified to happen in the next few years. How do we organise such a response, Ms Jones? Where do we lay down the humanitarian aid? Do we turn the whole of Texas, New Mexico, Arizona, and Florida into one great refugee camp? And then, don't forget, in a few decades, we'll have to move these camps north because our own southern states will start to become climate disasters themselves? Do you think, in the end, Canada can take a billion or more climate refugees?"

Annabelle couldn't believe any of this.

"Do you see my problem?" The president seemed exhausted but kept talking. "It's too late to fix the climate between the tropics now. Crop failure, as you know, is the norm. People will need to evacuate sooner or later – not just Mexico and Indonesia – but everyone who lives in the middle parts of the Earth.... And, as I just explained, because of the sinking of Jakarta, things have started a little early in Indonesia. The people who are affected can move further south, or further north. And because of the conditions of the city's collapse, this particular crowd of tens of millions of people can only move south. And once they get started, stopping them becomes increasingly impossible. They will be driven by starvation, heat, and thirst – millions of them, tens of millions and then the whole 150 million that make up Java will be on the move. Urban collapse will trigger further urban collapse. Jakarta could barely accommodate the people it did. Even now supply lines can't keep up – even with the amount of aid we can send – it doesn't matter. They don't want our money anymore. We can't pay them off. They can't harvest dollars and eat them. We could give them all the money they wanted if they stayed where they are – but they just can't eat cash, they can't drink it. They want food – and that's what we don't have for them...."

He continued with a relentless tranche of facts: “And what about the United States? Population of Mexico City? Nine million – where do they go when the food stops being shipped in? They rush our way. But we have to stop them from moving north or they will seriously interrupt our own food lines. The experts have been studying this for two decades now. We will soon have to deploy the most extreme plan because it is getting too late to do anything else. A radioactive wasteland will help them decide to stay where they are, or it will kill them if they get too close – or it will force them to trek south...which is what we want.”

“Jesus Christ.” Annabelle put her head in her hands. She was descending into a state of shock. “How can anyone come up with plans like these? Nuke Mexico...” She shook her head slowly and found it hard to breathe.

“We don’t do it to be macabre Ms. Jones – but the world as it is – well, it is very close to being beyond saving – not as a whole anyway – and we have to seriously consider how we can start saving ourselves, our own nations, our own cultures and way of life. What else is there? This is the only issue Australia has to face – and no one in Canberra can bring themselves to make a decision.”

“You’re going to cauterise us as well?”

“No...but this brings me to my problem” He clicked his pen again as he waited for her to look at him. “Do you see the small metal drawer under the console in front of you?”

“Yes.”

“Open it up.”

Annabelle stood, went over to the drawer and put her hand on the handle.

“What do you see?”

Annabelle pulled open the drawer and stared a long time at what was in the drawer. Her role in this nightmare was starting to become clear to her. She could barely reply to the question, but in the end, she said: “I see three keys on three brass tags”

“Read out the tags, Annabelle”

She didn't want to touch them but could see letters on the tags. She read them out. "One has 'PO'"

"That's 'Panel Operational'"

"Another has 'PTF'"

"That's 'Permission to Fire"

"The last one has 'Fire Inhib/Enbl'"

"And that one is the 'Firing Inhibited/Enabled' key."

"But why are they here?

The President was dry in his explanation of what she could do next. "If you take those three keys and insert them into the three keyholes in front of you, turn them on and press the firing buttons underneath each keyhole, you will launch a nuclear attack against Indonesia. Two dozen or so nuclear warheads will land across the south of the island of Java, West Irian, Papua, and New Guinea. If you press them, the north of Australia will be cauterised. You will be safe. The Australian way of life will be secured.

He clicked his pen again, slowly and in desperation. "If you press those buttons, you will cauterise the entire northern frontier of your country for decades to come. A great nuclear wasteland will umbrella Australia right across your northern neighbours. It will insure you against major population movements from Asia. Coming south will not be an option. The fleet of boats that are poised to hit your shores may start arriving even this week. If you press those buttons now, their Armada will be destroyed before it is launched. The island of Java – and a range of other northern islands will become uninhabitable. You will be the saviour of Australia – not from a military invasion, but from an unarmed, well-planned, swamping by millions of innocent and desperate people seeking food and drink.

"If you turn those keys and press those buttons, your Australian lifestyle will go on unaffected. You'll have enough water to drink for your 20-odd million, your food bowls of Victoria and Tasmania will still make enough for you, – hell – you can even keep on mining that damned coal you all love so much. And ironically, the nuclear clouds caused by the attack may even slightly decrease planetary temperature for a time...."

The shock had sent Annabelle into automatic pilot. She just mumbled "What a problem you face."

The President shook his head at her. "I can't bring myself to do it Ms. Jones. I am weak willed and I have received no guidance from Canberra. I have come to the view that we should let it all unfold – and see if 150 million people really can land in Australia – if they can be accommodated by you in your cities and your homes... It is an experiment that the humanitarian in me wants to watch play out. But, before it all ends that way, I wanted to see what *you* thought..."

She had no idea what to think. "You're going to let it happen?"

His face was full of genuine sadness. "I am, I'm afraid – and so too is Canberra. We all feel the alternative – Cauterisation – is the end of the world as we know it... but... there are some who feel you need to be given a chance..."

"What chance is that?" Annabelle felt her soul leaving her body, her mouth now just talking to be polite.

"*You're* the chance Annabelle – you have the keys – you can fire if you want. I have chosen you to be the conscience of your country. You get to act; you get to choose."

"Are you fucking insane? Destroy all of Java – just to save ourselves? That's barbaric, that's insane, that's worse than the Nazis. I won't do it, no one could do it..."

As she was shouting at the screen, her analysist's mind kicked in. "But... what if I don't do it?"

The President was resolute in his cold matter-of-factness. "Then, I have two Marine landing craft approaching the coast just north of where you are. When the great Armada of refugee boats arrive in Australian waters, the entire north of your country will descend into chaos – so we need to get our warheads out. The Marines are accompanied by nuclear weapons experts. They will ensure the silos become inoperative and they will transport the important stuff back to the United States. If you don't fire, I'm afraid Australia will be left to fend for itself. I can't leave U.S. nuclear warheads in amongst all the chaos that I know is coming your way…"

Annabelle slammed shut the drawer. "We will get help, I'm sure of it!"

The President smiled in agony to himself, overwhelmed by what he had to put into words… and then after a pause said – "Can I tell you something I shouldn't?"

"Sure. Why not – how can this get worse?"

"When we asked your Prime Minister what he thought he could do – he came up with a plan…"

"Which was?" Annabelle asked suspiciously.

"Set up an Australian Government in exile and relocate it to Hawaii."

"You're joking."

"Well, they considered New Zealand for a time, but eventually settled on Hawaii. So, no, I'm not joking. If you don't press those buttons – the head honchos in Canberra are going to get themselves a plane out of there and direct the response from the other side of the Pacific. Maybe the New Zealanders will pitch in and try to help you. Maybe all 25 million of your fellow Australians can retreat to the South Island as the Indonesians swamp you. And if that's the help you think you will need to fix all this – then go ahead and believe it – but I'm asking you to be realistic. The United States can help you now. The help we offer is – you are right – monstrous, but it will work. Oh, and when I say we can help you "now" – I mean the next few hours… after that I will have to order the decommissioning of the site you are standing in."

The click of his pen emphasised his words.

She was incredulous. "Hours? Are you joking?"

"We thought the Indonesian Armada would be setting off over the next few months. But because the weather is so good this week– and the forecasts suggest it is very good – it could be that in less than two hours or so the first convoys will launch. By tonight enough boats will be far enough off the coast that they will escape being destroyed by any nuclear blast. We can't bomb the sea. Those nuclear weapons you have only work on land…"

"But the United Nations..." She almost screamed at the screen.

"The Chinese are occupied with plans to shift their southern populations north. India is doing the same while battling horrendous droughts and crop failures – you might have read about the inhuman conditions in Chennai and Kerala at the moment – and all because of food restrictions – and, of course, we don't know what the Russians are doing... which is usual. The English – well, perhaps now you can see what Brexit was really about. We can't work out how Western Europe can be saved – it's too well connected to Africa, the Middle East, and the Near East to be "cauterisable". NATO thinks conventional policing may save the continent. But at least the British can cauterise themselves from the continent by using nuclear missiles. They are considering a launch from their Trident submarines in the next year or so. They aim to turn Normandy, Breton, and Holland into nuclear wastelands – sadly... it's a plan complicated by the fact that the French are also nuclear armed and might retaliate...."

Listening to all this Annabelle was suddenly livid. "So, cauterisation is not even about saving the West – it's about saving the English-speaking West? Is that the only definition of civilization you can work with?" She could see by his reaction that he hadn't even thought of that, so she pressed on "And why me. Why am I here? Why can't you do this? Or our fucking lame-arse Prime Minister?"

He held out his hands towards the screen trying to calm her. "Because this is the first step in our cauterisation program...." He couldn't finish the sentence. He put his hands down and his pen back in his pocket. Then he ran his fingers through his hair knowing how difficult the next few words would be. "You're right, it is a brutal and inhuman move, and we have to take the first step very carefully. It's a program that, we suspect, will not be received well on the international stage – we – that is, your Prime Minister and I – thought it would be best if, in the first instance, it could be perceived as an accident." He stared at her waiting for her to understand what he meant.

It took her a few moments. "Oh fuck – I'm your accident!"

"Yes, you are."

CHAPTER 15

The Patriarchy Rides Again...

Annabelle was suddenly jolted out of her shock by the suggestion that she would accidently nuke Indonesia.

"Fuck you!" she shouted at the screen. "Fuck you, you evil piece of shit – what are you going to tell the world? – That I bumped the buttons with my big dumb female arse? – or that I pressed the firing buttons thinking that they'd turn on the light for the make-up mirror? Fuck you...and fuck you again, you patriarchal piece of shit!"

The President was suddenly backtracking. "No... hell no, this is not about female technological incompetence – in fact we're going to sell it as 'Australia's leading investigative journalist stumbles upon nuclear secret – but accident occurs.' Look, I've got a mock-up of the front page of the *Sydney Morning Herald* here, this is what it will look like..."

Here he held up to the screen a very good likeness of the front page of the Sydney paper. The headline read:

INDONESIAN NUCLEAR ATTACK:
Journalist Discovers Secret Australian Nuclear Arsenal
Trigger Inadvertently Pressed

"You write the *Herald* in Washington now?" Annabelle asked caustically.

The president's face reappeared from behind the sheet of newsprint – "Wouldn't be the first time... Actually, this is a prop we used in our planning scenarios."

"You've been planning all this – and you still couldn't avoid killing tens of millions? And now I have to take the blame because none of you fucking piss-weak little men have the guts to own this..."

The President was still consoling her. "You can put it that way – but if we sell it as an accident, we can avert possible nuclear retaliation from Russia, China – we can't guarantee their reactions without you... without this seeming to be somewhat *unplanned.*"

Annabelle could only build on her outrage. "And did you think about what happens to me after all this – are you going to kill me?"

"If we were going to kill you, we would have done it already Ms. Jones. We could have left your body there on the floor, launched the missiles and blamed you anyway. But as I said – this is something I am averse to doing. Why? Because I don't know. I don't want to make this decision. It's not a *fait accompli* – if you don't press those buttons, then, nothing will happen. Your living presence here is about giving Australia a chance. It is a cold thing to say – but if you can't bring yourself to do it, then I will respect your decision. But that's it, we can't, we won't be bailing you out... and I will assess the world's reaction to what is about to happen and that might help me make a decision about Mexico..."

"So, you're giving Australia a chance – but not Indonesia..."

The President ignored this, by closing his eyes for a moment to let it pass, and then added: "And we shan't be murdering you because one day this will all come out – the decision you were presented with – but it won't be without some suffering on your part.... I know I will be condemned by history... and I think now, whatever you choose, press, or don't press, you will be condemned along with me. Either way, the moment you came into this room, we were both headed for infamy."

Annabelle was now terrified at a whole new level. "I know why you're letting me live – because it looks more plausible. Kill me and the conspiracy junkies would be even more rabid. Let me live and it looks all so fucking plausible. You fucking calculating piece of shit...What happens to me now? What happens if I just walk out – and 'one day' it comes out that I could have saved my nation – but I didn't?"

"I must face the same question. All I know is that when you leave here, whatever you do, you'll get arrested for trespassing. You'll get handed over to the Australian Federal Police – maybe you'll get a slap on the wrist, maybe you'll get shipped to The Hague to stand trial for Crimes Against Humanity, I don't know... but none of the jurisdictions or the courts you might face can execute you – not even the Hague. In the worst case, you'll end up in a very nice prison somewhere. And... I suppose you'll become reviled, your name will become a by-word for stupidity, or evil, and, disturbingly, you'll probably become a hero for a number of right-wing lunatics and white supremacists when they work out you acted willingly to press those buttons... And, let me warn you, if you tell anyone about this conversation, I suspect most people will think you've become delusional – because we will be denying it at this end." He took the pen out of his pocket again and clicked it... "But when the details of the cauterisation program leak out. Or when I am finally forced to nuke Mexico, people will see the pattern emerge – when I have to do that, then people will get it that you were a pawn in all this... that you were our patsy. That you were the first one of us to step forward and save Western Civilization. Your reputation will rise from the..." He stopped himself by clicking his pen once more.

"...from the tomb like Jesus? Or from the ashes of Indonesia?"

He winced and reassured her: "Any individual's name is a very little thing in the face of the great question we must now confront..."

"Which is?"

"Ok. This is it. Are you ready? The question of questions: 'Is Western Civilization worth saving?' Should our way of life be preserved at the expense of a dying world? Or should we all go down together? Which is, truly, the only other option now...."

He stopped for a moment to let this sink in. "Let me give you one argument for why I think it is worth saving – why I think you should consider pressing those buttons and saving what we have. You remember a little while ago I mentioned that I got the chance last week to invite a Wayang Kulit *dalang* to the White House – Asep Sunadar?"

"Yes"

"Well, he's still here. I haven't let him go home. Not just yet. He's one of 12,000 prominent Indonesians that our universities have invited to stay and work in the United States this year. This was also part of our planning. And don't forget – there's a substantial Indonesian community in Australia – about 100,000. 20,000 in Canada, another 200,000 American Indonesians here in the States. Now all these people will keep the Bahasa language and Indonesian culture alive no matter what happens to Java. And how many other cultures of the world will be saved and protected in the multicultural suburbs of Sydney and California, Melbourne and Chicago, Montreal, and New York if we act now? Think of the Australian Indigenous culture you'll be preserving by pressing those buttons. And think of the heritage and the ideals of Ancient Greece and Rome, the legacy of the French and American Revolutions, the British rule of law, Westminster democracy, merit in political advancement – should all that be just tossed into the chaotic swill that's about to engulf the world, or is *some* of it worth saving?"

Annabelle was beyond understanding how the whole of Western Civilization was now somehow at the mercy of what her fingers did next. "I suppose you're really just assuming that I will fire these bloody missiles because I am, deep down, just like you – some kind of evil fucking cultural supremacist?"

The President slumped wearily in his chair. "Isn't everyone on the planet a cultural supremacist of some kind? Wouldn't we all nuke the world for our own way of life? But really – I've told you what I think, and that's it. It is you who are the one unknown in all this – that's why I am having this long and detailed conversation with you Annabelle. That's why you are not being confronted by some general barking orders down the screen at you, or some political functionary trying to blackmail you into doing what you do not want to do. It's me – the steadfast yet sympathetic face of Western civilization itself... and, I'll admit it again Ms. Jones, even I am not exactly sure what you should do. At heart, I am also confused as hell about this. I am also sickened by the thoughts of what I might be called on to do. Do you really think I want to put our cauterisation program into operation? All I know is that we have a planet that already does not function as it should. Crops in the tropics will not grow because of the excesses of global overheating that we, each of us, failed to stop. Life has become impossible in the mid-regions of the globe. It's too hot and dry to support life, and the people in those regions will be left to die if they don't move themselves. And they will move. Crops aren't growing, drinking water is disappearing, sea levels are rising. If they stay put, they die. So, they are not staying put. They are being sane and rational and getting on the move – and in the hundreds of thousands. Soon it will be in the millions. And they are headed towards you. What do you do? Sacrifice it all, let it all go to hell? Or save a bit of it – the bit where you live, the bit where you grew up? I don't know..."

He was shaking a little. From fear or anger, Annabelle couldn't tell. "I put you in this scenario because what we have to work with is your sense of humanity, your sense of social justice... I can see it clearly. It is there in everything you have ever written – and we're going to work with that... if you choose not to fire those weapons – then *we* have other plans – but Australia will have lost its chance to join us in our cauterised ark... Someone in Australia has to make the call and everyone in Canberra is too shit scared. You are not given to fear, your writing has shown how brave you are. Your country needs you – and you have to make this decision now."

Annabelle slumped into a chair. "Why me?" she asked, almost to herself.

The President shifted in his chair. "But there's a dark side too. One that we have also calculated in our strategies. Can I tell you about *your* dark side Ms. Jones...?"

Her head slumped onto her chest. She refused to answer him.

"What we have in our favour is that you are an Australian – a white one – one who grew up listening to an incessant and deeply xenophobic rhetoric about boats, about the north. You may have pushed all that away from you – but it was there, ringing in your ears your whole life long. You are a citizen who has been told that the boats must be stopped – that the country must remain integral, Western, a satellite of the UK or the US, and never Asia. If you press those buttons, then it is simply a gesture that will become a continuation of the policy, by other means, that justifies your offshore detention centres, your national xenophobia, your inherent fears... These missiles, sitting there, waiting for your command, you know what? They really *will* stop the boats..."

The President searched the monitor in front of him for any sign that she was being affected by his words. "The other thing in our favour, Ms. Jones, is that you are the child of generations of white Australians who have been fed from infancy on the idea that a great "yellow" peril will descend from the north and swamp you – and the irony now is that this great mythic fear, an unjustified fear for so long is now – under the new heat of global warming – a reality. You are indeed about to be swamped from the north. And there are three keyholes and three keys, and three buttons in front of you who will tell us who you really are Annabelle. Are you the world citizen who's ready to abandon your way of life and your civilization to feed the last mouths of a dying species? Or are you, underneath all your social justice sentiments, just another multi-generational, hyper-xenophobic girl from the land down under?"

"You fucking prick," was all she could say.

"Admit it, that is exactly your heritage. And if you don't admit it, then maybe you won't make the clearest decision..."

"I won't admit it. I'm better than that, and if you want my fucking final answer, then I won't do this. I refuse to blow up 150 million people and destroy a nation. I can't do it. No human should ever be able to even think up this shit, let alone actually carry it out. I refuse. Completely and utterly. Bring on your marines – dismantle these warheads. Get them the fuck out of here... They should never have been put here in the first place... We didn't fight two world wars because we're not up for a challenge. We have the resolve to work with this. We will take them in, we will feed them, we will not dare to turn from this task! No matter what the cost... We will be human first, and only then Australian..."

The President smiled. "The Michael Mackintosh Foot option hey?"

He shook his head with a deep sadness. "Do you remember I started all this by speaking about Foot. He, and Neil Kinnock, and Jeremy Corbyn – and all those brave, brave women of Greenham Common – remember them – God bless their ghosts every one of them. Each a great advocate for nuclear disarmament. And they were wrong then. The Russians had the bomb – so we needed the bomb. Everything was in perfect balance and the world rolled along. But the ghost of Michael Foot is right now, more correct than ever. When the Wall fell in '89, we should have got rid of these things – but it is too late now. By God, in the long run, Foot and Kinnock, Corbyn, and Sanders... they were all completely correct. Disarm, dismantle. But..." he sighed long and sadly, "no one acted... and now we have these great tools of war... but it is not for war that we will use them, but for the vary basics of national survival..."

He stood up and the camera shifted upwards to follow him. "On the other side of the Cold War, and with a planet falling towards hell, nuclear weapons take on another importance, another use. And we didn't see it coming until recently... We should have disarmed even before we began the nuclear age. But the Cold War... God! How the hell did we get through the Cold War without a single nuclear weapon being fired in anger? And once that was over, we should have disarmed. Not me, not Michael Foot, no one thought nuclear weapons would be the answer to our future in this way now – but these catastrophic tools are all we have left, and it is the only option we have left to take – bomb around our own borders and spend our final days in the nationalistic bubbles that these blasts will provide..."

"You fucking prick." Now she was mumbling... catatonic... saying over and over "...you fucking prick..."

"Now that the world has descended into its current state, those buttons look less inhuman if they are our salvation and not the start of a mutually assured destruction. They might save some of us. Who would have thought it – we are about to enter the age of nuclear salvation...

"Those nations who have nuclear weapons are those who might survive longest against the forces of climate change and the insane chaos it is starting to produce – that it is producing this very second. And you are in this position only because John "Eyebrows" Howard and George "Dubya" Bush thought ahead – those two great war crime cretins stumbling about looking for any excuse to invade Iraq – they actually did something useful. Who would have guessed...? They gave you this option Ms. Jones. Well, in your case right now, maybe having these weapons is damnable. But the great heroes of Baghdad engineered this chance for you... and in a way you are right to turn it down.... In some way I was hoping you would turn it down. You are taking the crazier option; you are making a strangely humane stance and I respect that... I respect it very much."

He clicked his pen again with a sad rhythm, then continued. "If you had pressed those buttons – you would have been our patsy, but also my guinea pig. We would have been able to judge how the world would react – this would have given us more info on how to proceed with our own cauterisation program here in North America. But... Australians never were innovators – only ever followers. In less than a year, perhaps only in a few months, I will have to make this decision too Ms. Jones. I hope I have your clarity of vision and your steely resolve...but I suspect not. I suspect I will be forced to act merely as a pawn of history... Anyway – let me be undiplomatic and say this – your decision not to do this was far clearer and more precise than any decision I was able to get out of Canberra. So, thank you for that."

"Now, it is way past my bedtime, and I am very weary. What will happen next is that a clock will appear in your room there – can you see it?" He clicked his pen impatiently.

Over the door Annabelle noticed a clock in red numerals appear. It read "120." The President explained "That will count down 120 minutes. Two hours. That's about the time it will take to get personnel organised to come and collect you. It is also when we need to give the final order for our Marines to land and dismantle the warheads.... Because of the remarkable weather this afternoon, I suspect, the Armada will start moving off soon... maybe tonight. But, while the clock is ticking, you can still change your mind. I give you that final chance. When the clock gets to zero, the control centre you are in will shut down and go offline. The door will unlock. And there'll be some military police waiting outside to get you back to Canberra."

He clicked his pen one last time. "And may the Lord God have mercy on your soul and on the soul of every Australian who will have to face what is to come. It will be true chaos. Thank you for your attention and your patience Ms. Annabelle Jones, it has been a strange and unfortunate delight in meeting you and I am so sorry that it was under these horrendous circumstances that we spoke."

And with those words, the screen went blank.

III

A canoe

CHAPTER 16

A Cup of Tea

The room went black for a moment, and Annabelle swayed on her feet for a time not knowing what to do. Then a cold green light illuminated the room. A few moments after the large screen went dead, Annabelle heard a trembling close to her – she went for her backpack and dug out her mobile - "Now you give me phone reception, you bastards!" She looked at the ceiling. "I know you're listening...."

She looked through the number of calls that had come in. Michael had tried to get through three times. She wanted to speak to her husband but figured there'd be time for that later. She really wanted to speak to Black Veil. She really thought he would know what to do – even though she couldn't trust him, he was still the reason she was here. He was the reason she was thinking this way. She needed external confirmation of what was going on. Her editor had called twice but she ignored everyone and put through an international call through to Seth Ryan. Seth was a good friend of hers and the ABC's South-East Asia correspondent. He answered straight away.

"Seth, its Annabelle Jones."

"Annabelle!" – his came booming voice down the line, the screech of moped horns wailing away behind him. It was the noise of the outside world and Annabelle drank it in.

"Seth, listen – the clock is against me" she looked at the figures above the door. "What's going on in Jakarta – someone said the city is sinking and there's a mass exodus?"

He was emphatic – "It's not sinking Annabelle – it's sunk – 10 million people are fleeing the city, seawater up to their knees. It's complete chaos..."

She was confused. "Why aren't we getting this on the news?"

"I have no fucking idea – and it's been driving me mad... No one wants to hear about the environment, and bloody no one wants to hear about Indonesia – so put those two topics together and Australians can't stop yawning... No one could care less."

"Are you in Jakarta?"

"Fuck no, I was there this morning. They've pulled me back to Singapore. They know it's serious – but not serious enough to run my stories. Maybe its climate fatigue – maybe its Indonesia's long-standing irrelevance to all Australians – but to me it looks like the biggest story of the year – but no one in News agrees with me – there's been a bit about it in the *Guardian* – but that's it for mainstream..."

"Listen..." Annabelle desperately wanted to know about the boats, "... when you were there did you hear rumours about boats – lots of boats setting out for Australia?"

"Yeah, yeah, I did – rumours though. I toured a few southern port towns – lots of people moving about – a hell of a lot of boats moored – being spruced up – they were looking in good condition. I asked about them. Someone told me there was a fishing festival coming up and that's why they were all primed. But I didn't see any boats setting out to fish..."

Annabelle explained to him: "I've heard that they're all setting out at once. That way they can force their way past Australian naval defences..."

"Really?" Seth sounded shocked but not surprised. "I mean that would make sense – it could be happening – everything is there for it to happen – and a fuck-load of tension on the streets – a lot of violence against the northern Javanese who've been on the move south.

That's why they got me out – the whole place – I mean all of Java – seems on the edge of complete collapse – the drought is really fucking the place over. I saw starving children... god... you don't want to know what I saw..."

"Listen – those boats – could they be sailing tonight? I mean what's the weather like?"

"I'm outside Raffles. I'm looking at the sea right now – it's the calmest night I've seen in months – but there's a strong breeze – its heading South-east – so, yeah, if you were trying to sail from Java to Australia, that would make the conditions perfect. Fuck it Annabelle – do you think that's happening? I mean tonight?"

"My source says 'probably'."

Seth's voice was overwhelmed with emotion. "Shit... is it a good source?"

"Untested, but official," said Annabelle.

"Right. Thanks for the lead – I'm going to call some Indonesian friends – see what's up... will get back to you..." There was a click and the line went dead.

Annabelle took what he said to be corroboration...

Like an emotional zombie, she got off the chair she'd collapsed into after the President signed off. She paced the room. She looked at the clock – 100 minutes left - and eventually slid down the wall opposite the great door and sat on the floor. She was thinking what to do next. She pressed a number on her phone and listened to the ring tone. A woman's voice answered.

"Hello darling – how is your trip going?"

"Hi Mum," Annabelle said wistfully, almost vacantly, "what are you doing?"

"Just had dinner with your father – waiting for the kettle to boil so we can have a nice cup of tea..."

"Would murder the entire world for a cup of tea right now..."

Her mother read the subtext. "You don't seem your usual self, dear – what's up?"

"Mum – hey – I've got a hypothetical question for you – are you listening?"

"Yes dear, go ahead."

"What if you knew boats were coming – thousands of boats with thousands of refugees on them all setting off in one night – maybe hundreds of thousands of refugees aboard – all of them unarmed – all of them hungry and thirsty – and they're about to land on the north coast and make their way through the country by any means they can – and there's too many of them to stop or shoot – what would you do?"

"Hang on dear – I'll ask your father."

"No! Mum! Fuck!" Annabelle was annoyed – she wanted her mother's opinion not her father's. In the background she could hear her mother repeating the hypothetical. She heard him grumble something then her mother was back on the line. "Hello dear – I've spoken to your father and we both think a 'Brisbane Line' would be best."

That made no sense: "What's a 'Brisbane Line', Mum?"

"During the war – when we were fighting the Japs – the government invented the concept of the Brisbane Line – you basically draw a line from Brisbane across the country and you destroy everything north of that line. I think it's originally a Russian idea – you know – when Napoleon marched on Moscow... how many sugars dear?" She heard her mum shout to her dad before coming back on the line. "They just burnt the place to the ground and Napoleon's troops starved to death. See, you let the invaders come on in – and then make sure they starve to death in the wastelands you create – or possibly let them set up their own gerrymandered democracy and watch them drown in their own corruption – which is a good definition of Queensland if you ask me..." Annabelle could barely wait while her mother laughed at her own little joke.

"Seriously mum – if you had nuclear weapons what would you do?"

Annabelle heard some more mumbling. "Your father says 'nuke the thirsty bastards to hell – it's not like we've got any water left in the Murray-Darling anyway... or any fish. And I agree with him – press all the buttons and just get rid of them. You know your nephew, little

Jonathan? He's starting kindergarten next week – how will he get to kindergarten if the streets are full of thirsty boat people screaming for food?"

"Gee – thanks for the comforting advice, Mum..." Annabelle was distraught at the casual way they thought about nuking the world. She put on a fake cheery voice. "Anyway, I gotta go – save a cuppa for me – see you soon – bye."

Annabelle pressed another number. The phone rang and her school friend Stella answered. "Hi Stella, it's Annabelle..."

"Are you safe?" her friend asked.

"I am safe – at the moment. Listen, listen real hard. I'm in a nuclear bunker, and there's three buttons in front of me and if I push them, Indonesia gets wiped off the face of the earth... which is great for us because at this moment a couple-of-hundred-thousand, maybe several million starving Indonesians are getting ready to sail towards us to save their own lives – so, question – do I press the buttons? I need a clear mind to talk me through this."

Stella gave nothing but stunned silence. Annabelle waited while her friend tried to work out what she had just said. "Stella?" She asked wondering if the line had gone dead. Finally her voice came on the line, "So – your trip up there – it was trap? They're asking you to you nuke Indonesia?"

"No Stella, that's the worst bit...they're not forcing me to do anything. I can just do nothing, and we get to be the new Java, or...or I can press the buttons and we'll be safe and hated. What would you do?"

"Aren't we hated anyway?" Stella asked rhetorically. Then she paused and added, "hang on – why you – why do you have to make the choice?"

Annabelle wearily mumbled down the phone – "because if I press the buttons, they'll write it off as an unfortunate accident... I get to take the rap on what is perhaps the most heinous thing a civilisation can do – wipe out a whole *other* civilisation, wipe out millions... Mass genocide done this time by a stumbling over-curious journalist, whose fat arse sat on the firing keys ..."

"Isn't that what all history's been about..." Stella interrupted.

"What? Fat arses and accidents?"

"No," Stella said. "Civilizations destroying each other? Survival of the fittest? You want my advice? How dare they put you in this situation – can't you just tell them to go fuck themselves?"

"I'm the only one in the room – it's been sealed off. I'm the only one who can fire the missiles in time. Anyway – don't worry about logistics – I just want to know what to do? I mean, what would you do? You're a bigger bleeding heart than me, Stella – you're the humane socialist of all socialists – tell me we can do it – tell me we can rise to the challenge of saving these unarmed and desperate millions as they stream down towards us. Reassure me that it is possible – that Australia can make itself into Asia's great refugee camp?"

Annabelle waited in silence for a good minute before Stella replied. "I think, Annabelle, the world is fucked. It's too late to play the international charity-giver. I don't think we can save the world – I'm not even sure we can even save ourselves... Press them, press all their fucking buttons and I'll be here to comfort you when it's over..."

She was stunned by Stella's certainty. "Fuck! Really? Who are these people..." Annabelle was overcome by a raw and uncontrolled anger. She threw her phone across the room. It smashed against one of the concrete walls. She immediately realised what a stupid thing she had done and ran after it. "No, no, no, no, no, NO!" She put it to her ear – but it was dead. She began beating herself over the head with her fists. "Stupid, stupid girl" she screamed at herself. "Why would you do that..."

She slumped back onto the floor, nursing her broken phone. She saw that she only had 80 minutes left. She had no idea what to do. She just sat there. She waited, mesmerised. She looked again. Now the clock read 70. She took out a handkerchief and wrapped it around the phone like it was a swaddling cloth, rocking her phone like it was a baby. She stayed silent for a long time.

Then she started shouting. "I know you can hear me," she screamed at the walls. "I know you are watching. You can see inside my brain can you? Look at this!" She said holding her phone aloft wrapped in its handkerchief – "This was me when I was young... I'd wrap anything up and nurse it – sick birds, the cat, my dolls, my brother – all of them wrapped tightly and securely. When my parents asked me what I wanted to be when I grew up, I told them 'Universal Mother' – fucking hell... I actually said that – 'Universal Mother.' I wanted to be a mother to everything and everyone. And now look at me – how can a mother, a Universal Mother, destroy anything, and I'm thinking about killing millions? I can't do it." And at that she slumped over on the floor rocking back and forth, holding her broken baby.

The clock ticked on.

CHAPTER 17

Idea of the Self

After a few moments she woke from her daze with a new resolve. "Ok, I can work this out myself." Annabelle told herself out loud. She sat up and looked at the clock – she had less than an hour. She didn't care who could hear her as she mumbled away to herself and the dull concrete corners of the room. "Who am I? I am a unit which is one-eight-billionth of the human species. The species forms webs of intricate and sophisticated cultures across the face of the planet.... But the planet is sick. Its tropical zones are the most populous and the sickest. Can the billions who inhabit the areas between Capricorn and Cancer be saved from the heat, the famine, the droughts, the disease ...?

"We move them beneath the Brisbane Line – and things become worse, hotter, nastier and the planet heats more. So, then we form another line – the Sydney Line – and we move everyone that we can south of that – the planet keeps getting warmer – then, we make a Melbourne Line – then we move everyone – how many? To Tasmania, to New Zealand.... Then to the melted and newly exposed grasslands of Antarctica? Can we survive there? 30 million Australians, plus 150 million Javanese, and probably half a million Polynesians – they'll need saving too... New Zealanders? Maybe they'll be fine, but everyone else will need saving...

"Ok, ok, I've got it" – she got two of the chairs and lay them down on the floor upside down. She made them into something looking like a boat. She sat between them and started rowing. "Right, now, I'm in the boat. Maybe it's a canoe. We've all done this, haven't we....? At primary school, high school, and we're doing it again – that exercise – you know there's 8 billion people in the boat with you and you have to decide who to keep and who to send overboard? And you're sailing to a new world that needs to be restarted...But you can't take everyone. Who do you keep? You've got to keep the doctor, the scientist, the nurse, the poet, the lawyer, the tool-maker, and the Universal Mother, the Wayang Kulit puppeteer, the Imam – who goes, who stays? We've all done this exercise Annabelle – time to do it again." She paddled for a moment, then shouted at herself "Do it, fucking work it out, and do it, make an answer..."

She hit herself on the head again to try to get her thoughts in line. "Do it, do it. Work it out. So, do we kick Indonesia out of the boat? What is it? A series of Islands, Muslim, Chinese, Hindu, Christian – no great scientists, no great universities, no Universal Mothers... how do you rebuild the world just using Indonesia? Will it work? But then what would the cosmos look like without Indonesia? History, think about history – the Dutch needed it for spices, then the Japanese took it, then independence, then we helped the Americans set up a dictatorship under Suharto, slaughter, then independence again – and now that its unarmed people threaten us... We nuke it without a single thought. Bullshit. Stop the boats – the ultimate Tony Abbot solution – nuke the very idea of a boat...poor Indonesia – what did it ever do to us? How colonial is all this? But how will they live if they come here...? How many cups of tea will we need? They should kill us all for being such arseholes. Perhaps we deserve this? Perhaps this is our punishment. Perhaps the Universal Mother should be escorted off the boat and left for dead... Indonesian children can live. Live on without her... they have their own mothers"At this thought she strted crying.

She realised what Australia would become if it took on all these people. "A Commonwealth of trauma, homesickness... Maybe that's who we always were – I mean what is 'Australia'? How big is it? Can it be the whole world?"

"Ah, now, maybe this is the answer." Annabelle stood up and got out of her boat and whispered to the walls. "Maybe we always were crypto-fascists and agents of genocide. If we had to eradicate indigenous culture in order to live here, maybe that is a part of each one of us – we know how to do it – we already know how to kill millions... maybe that's why he asked me?"

She looked at her hands. "These fingers have always been able to press buttons like these buttons. Maybe only now I am seeing my secret self... maybe he's right – all white Australians would press these buttons, and I am that. It is inside me – no need to argue." She ran to the drawer that held the three keys. She picked them up and walked around the room with them. Gazing at them.

"Oh, shit. I have been so stupid..." Holding the keys high, she laughed and laughed again. "I bet you they don't even work! I bet you this is all a set up. IT'S A GAME! Is this like reality television? Or a Stanford Experiment – not Stanford, Milgram. It a Milgram? Hey? You can come out now, where's the compare? Where's the studio audience? I've worked it out. You got me, boy, did you get me! And I liked how you even got the President to come on – I can see why he'd want to be on a television show! I mean, after Trump everyone wants to be a reality TV star *and* the President simultaneously..."

She looked at the keys again. "I bet they don't even fit." She looked at the clock – only 20 minutes left. "Is this going out live? Have you cut to an ad break? I bet they don't even work. I bet, I bet..." At this she ran around to the panel and began inserting the keys. "Permission to Fire. Woo hoo! I've got permission to fire. As she turned the keys, new signs lit up beside the darkened screen:

SILO 1 – PREPARING TO LAUNCH. Then –
SILO 2 – PREPARING TO LAUNCH. And finally –
SILO 3 – PREPARING TO LAUNCH.

At this, the live video feeds of the silos moved from the peripheral screens to the large screen. The great water tanks at the Sewerage Works fell open into segments and ICBMs mounted on their slings rose up from out of the ground and swung around pointing to the North-East.

"Wow – great CGI on the missiles guys – is that animation? Or just old stock footage?"

Similarly, the screens that showed the rooves at the two sheds of the truck depots opened out and more missiles appeared in their slings, pointing at the skies ready to be fired. Annabelle was delighted. "Wow – great stage effects!" She peered closely at the screene "Are they models? Yes? They're really good models..."

She looked up and saw the signs, then watched the screens. Suddenly Annabelle was very sober. "That doesn't look like reality television, does it?"

She was certain she needed to get away from all this. "No, no, no – this is not right..." She got back into the imaginary canoe on the floor and tried to paddle away – "Got to leave now, got to get down steam... But there's no water now. No water...I can't paddle. Only dead fish! Billions of dead fish!" Her back was turned on the clock and the door. "Have to get out of here... I mean, I'm a human who believes in humanity. World government, international solutions, the world can work together to beat this or... maybe I'm just a shitty little moron like everyone else. Maybe the only thing we can expect from anyone... protect our own patch, our own pathetic right to self-gratification... our own way of life..." She stopped paddling for a moment to think. "Gliding along now, I am gliding across the dead fish and the dry river-bed, and everyone is waving to me from the banks.... They all love their Universal Mother..."

She felt a demon rise up from inside her. A demon that clearly saw the world as an 'us' and a 'them.' A demon who knew that no one was coming to help if we did not help ourselves. A demon that was sure they wouldn't help us if we were in trouble. She ran to the wall – as if it were a mirror, she started fixing her hair...

She kept explaining things to herself: "I mean, if I'm an Australian – how can I be me without Australia existing as it does? So, if I need to keep my 'self' as me, then surely my first duty is to protect my country above all things, so I can continue to be Annabelle Jones the *Australian*? Even if it means the destruction of the rest of the world? What weird fucking thinking is this? Where is it coming from?

"But if I don't press the buttons, I can't keep being me.... But – if I press the buttons, I will become the person who nuked Indonesia, the woman who *really* stopped the boats. Fuck you Tony Abbot. Smirking away as I watched my cartoons on Sunday morning. I am better than you... So much better than you...." She got back in her canoe and started rowing again...

"I AM THE WOMAN WHO, at last, CLOSED OUR REFUGEE CAMPS – I mean, after this why would we need refugee camps? Why would we need them if all refugees die of radiation sickness well before they leave....? I mean I am an Australian HERO! Right? Compassionate heart... After me, there can be no more refugees. I win, John Howard you disgusting fucking war criminal... You invaded Iraq because you bought the bullshit. I do this because I want to stay Australian and that's no bullshit. I beat you Tony Abbot – I do what you never could. Stop the boats, guaranteed...I'll stop the fucking boats."

At that, Annabelle put down her imaginary oars, got out of her imaginary canoe, and looked at the clock. There was two minutes to go. She walked zombie-like to the console.

She reached out her hand. But stopped.

"No," she told herself "I'm better than all this. I will be a mother. A Universal Mother. I will be the only mother for 150 million people. I alone will do it... come to me – all the children of the world! Come to me." She turned her head back towards the clock.

As it ticked down. She was relived at last that they had not got to her. It was all over, it was all safe. Everyone was safe. She was still the Universal Mother.

There was less than a minute to go. She breathed relief.

And yet...

In her mind's eye, she saw him clicking his pen. Again and again, he was able to push the button on his pen. He pushed it and each time he did, she felt, at a strange distance, vicariously, she felt the satisfaction he must have felt while he was clicking this pen. She knew this was the most pathetic reason in the world. But she also wanted to click a button as if it were a pen. She wanted to feel the click, feel the button driven home, feel the bliss of a thing done.

With less than 10 seconds on the clock, Annabelle Jones pressed the three launch buttons as though they were the button on a retractable pen.

The room was zapped of its energy, the lights flickered. On the screens, the missiles shot, one-by-one into the air. Dozens of them going up as if they had been thrown there in a game, hovering and about to fall back to earth - but then exploding into soaring flight. Going from some crazy slow start, then picking up speed in a way that would break your eyes. And as the satisfaction of pressing the buttons flooded from her fingers to her heart. Then other cameras showed the great trails of smoke fattening then dispersing through the skies.

She collapsed onto the ground and it all seemed to go dark around her. She trembled there, trying to sit up. She eventually got up and climbed into her imaginary canoe, hoping it was a funeral barge pushed out into a fjord. She linked her hands over her chest and lay there face up. She could see from the corner of her eyes that there were Vikings on the shore. Then men fired blazing arrows to set her barge alight and farewell her in a blazing, floating bonfire.

After a very long pause, a green light began flashing above the vault door. Slowly it moved open. At last, she could smell again the stale dank air that lingered in the hallway outside. And the heat. But she kept to her canoe.

After another long pause, two US Military Policemen entered the room. They told her to get up, but she couldn't stand. She was dead.

They asked her repeatedly to get up. She did not move but stayed in her imaginary canoe.

In the end they took one arm each and dragged her up. They took her from the room as she screamed for them to let her go. She insisted that they let her get back in her canoe. "I still have to work out who is coming and who needs to be put out of the boat! We need to make tea! A lot of tea!"

The two officers spent some time carrying her up the internal stairs. They laid her on a gurney when they got into the clinic upstairs. She looked at one of them. "Are you going to kill me now?"

One of them looked at her kindly and asked, "Why would we do that?"

Using the gurney, they were able to wheel her out the front door of the clinic. She felt that the gurney was like a canoe and settled again. When they came outside, she was half sitting up. There was a military police van parked in front of the clinic and the two officers directed the gurney towards it. They could have thrown her in the paddy of the back of the van. Instead, they made her comfortable in the back seat behind the front passenger's seat and drove towards the base. As the van drove down the main street, the citizens of the township were standing out in the open looking up in the sky and talking to each other – as if they were looking for fireworks in the late afternoon. The radio in the van was on.

"The is James Codrington with a Five P.M. News Update. Reports are coming in of a missile attack on Indonesia. Some reports say it is nuclear. This is yet to be confirmed. Observers presently have no idea from where the attack may have originated. We are crossing now to Seth Ryan who is phoning in from Singapore..."

Annabelle leaned forward and tapped one of the policemen on the shoulder. "I know Seth Ryan – he is a *good* journalist." She explained. "A *good* journalist reports the news, a good journalist does not become the news. I'm not a good journalist. I don't know..." She mumbled. Then she started speaking again. "But Seth will know... Seth will work it all out one day. Seth is a *good* journalist..." The policeman who had turned to face her nodded and turned his face forward again.

The van turned into the base. As they unloaded her from the van, Annabelle smiled to herself remembering the words of the President – that she would be a different person after she had left the room.

He was right. She was.

"I wonder what her name will be?" She asked the guards as they helped her out of the van. "You know... the person I will become?" She stopped and looked at the sky over the base. "I wonder what her story will be? I wonder how she will tell her story to herself...that story..." She looked at one of the police officers strangely, but kindly –

"Do you think her story will be convincing?

Compelling? Believable?

Do you?"

www.ingramcontent.com/pod-product-compliance
Lightning Source LLC
Chambersburg PA
CBHW060622310726
48982CB00003B/644

9780645728828